DOMNIȚA AND TUDOR AVĂDANEI

Novel

David Kimel

Domniţa and Tudor Avădanei

Novel
Copyright © 2025 David Kimel.

Published by: Paramount Book Publishing

Printed in the USA

To those who appreciate stories of past that remind us of the heroic times and places that are no more the same today.

Acknowledgment

It is said that gratitude is a virtue. I have many reasons to be grateful to a significant number of people who extended a helping hand in times of need, guiding me through moments of doubt, situations where every path seemed hopelessly blocked, or simply offering a much-needed word of encouragement

To my wife, Valeria, who has been my guiding light and life companion for the past 64 years and who has given me children whose love and devotion surpass any praise, I am deeply grateful for her understanding, trust in me, and the personal sacrifices imposed by life's circumstances. To her, I owe the peace and warmth of a home that has helped erase from memory the perennial hardships encountered beyond its walls.

Uprooted from the soil of the country that gave me life, I have strived to grow new roots in the welcoming land of Canada, where I knew no one and did not even speak the language of my new country. Yet, by the grace of Providence, I have achieved here what was not possible in my homeland—I have prospered and surrounded myself with family and friends. To all of them, I am profoundly grateful.

When time granted me the opportunity to lay my thoughts onto blank pages, through stories and images easily understood by any reader, I was met with the goodwill of true friends who encouraged my attempts, selflessly guided me toward success, and smoothed the transition from a technical career to a literary one. Among them, Mr. and Mrs. Dumitru Puiu Popescu, editors of the Romanian-language magazine Observatorul in Toronto, who allowed my writings be seen printed in their magazine. I owe it to them that, for nearly two decades, my articles have been regularly featured in the Subjective column.

Many other remarkable souls have supported me with encouragement, guidance, and advice, for which I remain deeply grateful, including writers Elena Buică, Veronica Pavel Lerner, the late Gavril Morariu, Daniela Cupşe Apostoaei, Codruţ Miron, and Leonard Voicu, who founded the Mihai Eminescu Literary Circle in Montreal for Romanian writers. To them, I owe my respect and deepest thanks.

This book, like the previously ones, are the collective product of individuals committed to bringing the works of lesser-known writers to life, taking on the risks of results that will only become clear over time. At Paramount Book Publishing, I had the pleasure of meeting people whose kindness, assistance, and guidance cannot go unnoticed: Joe Brandon, who had the patience and tact to dispel any uncertainty about entering an unfamiliar publishing process with institutions located hundreds of kilometers away; April Woods & Gary Miller, my Senior Project Managers and coordinator of this endeavor, whose warmth and dedication won me over; and the artists who designed the books cover, capturing the very essence of my novellas, I remain indebted.

Respect and sincere gratitude to all the individuals mentioned above and to the entire team at Paramount Book Publishing for bringing this book to life.

David Kimel

Contents

A Romanian Testimonial Book from the Land of the Maple Leaf

Across the Atlantic, in Canada, a vibrant Romanian literary life has long been taking shape—its representative character fueled by the large wave of emigration of sons and daughters from the Carpathians and the Lower Danube, who left long ago or more recently, in search of a safer and more prosperous life than the one left behind in the "lost homeland." Among those who departed for the "land of the maple leaf" is the man of letters, now a nonagenarian, David Kimel, whose roots lie in Bucharest, where he once studied at the renowned "Eminescu" School of Literature and Literary Criticism.

With a wealth of life experience dating back to his youthful years in Bucharest, Kimel emigrated in 1972 to Israel, and later settled permanently in Canada's bustling metropolis, Toronto—a city that not only offered him and his family a decent life but also gave him the opportunity to emerge as a writer. His literary journey began with contributions to Romanian-language and English-language journals, where he published his first volume of poems, *Simple Seeds*. From that debut to the book he has now entrusted to my attention, David Kimel has embarked on a veritable race against time, publishing—always well received by readers—novels, novellas, and travel memoirs (*From the Wide World*), with a tireless creative energy that seems to fuel his long and rich life.

As I said, David Kimel, trusting me, has submitted for consideration his latest novel, *Domnița and Tudor Avădanei*, freshly released from his creative workshop. This is a novel whose action unfolds against the backdrop of a pivotal historical transition—from 19th to 20th-century Romania—centered around two major military events: the Second Balkan War and the First World War. Its heroine, an emblematic figure, is Princess, and later Queen, Marie, accompanied by two other central characters: the schoolteacher Tudor Avădanei from the plains of Giurgiu, and the queen's beautiful lady's maid, Mura. Their love story, set against the apocalyptic backdrop of World War, moves the reader thanks to the writer's narrative mastery.

But what profoundly stirs the reader's awareness in this dual-natured novel—both historical and romantic—is David Kimel's thorough historical research regarding the Romanian royal family, particularly Queen Marie, as well as Romania's political life during *la belle époque*, and the tragedies endured by the Romanian people during the great conflagration of the First World War. All this serves as the background—a grand tapestry—upon which the deeply touching love story between Tudor and Mura is woven, under the wise and compassionate gaze of that "mother of the wounded," whom the Romanian people also saw as "Queen Marie the soldier," owing to her genuine and heartfelt involvement on the front lines of the War for National Unification. She was destined to become the first sovereign of Greater Romania.

Another secondary but significant character is Izu, a Jewish man for whom Tudor Avădanei shows heartfelt friendship and whom he defends from the antisemitic outbursts of a vulgar, militaristic comrade. Izu proves himself to be a good Romanian citizen, one who cherished his homeland and endured the horrors of war in her name.

One may confidently say that David Kimel's novel is a fresco of an entire era, a chronicle, if you will—vividly and convincingly rendered—marking him as a masterful novelist, one whose work proudly takes its place in the gallery of Romanian writers of the diaspora.

Prof. Dr. George Coandă

Member of the American Romanian Academy of Arts and Sciences, USA

Bringing Historical Events Closer

At a considerable distance in time, in a hyper-technologized world where the carousel of history seems to spin on entirely new coordinates and where humanity's fundamental value system performs dizzying pirouettes in its struggle to maintain a stable balance, speaking of history might, for some, seem outdated. Yet, it is the talent and skill of each writer that can captivate an audience, prompting reflection—whether the text touches on fiction or not.

One such writer is Mr. David Kimel, who masterfully demonstrates the art of bringing historical events closer to us, the readers. He knows how to animate and warm up the sepia-toned figures of the past, making historical data feel far from dry or lifeless. As if touched by a magic wand, we begin to hear voices, the gallop of horses, the hum of elegant salons, muffled cries from the battlefield, the rustle of taffeta, and the echo of famous lines.

With deep knowledge and thorough documentation, the author presents the events that shaped Romania from the late 19th to the early 20th century. He skillfully depicts the country's involvement in the Second Balkan War and the First World War, intertwined with the emblematic figure of Princess Missy—none other than the future Queen Marie.

With a confident hand, he alternates idyllic passages with scenes charged with tension and drama, crafting a moving and enchanting story centered around a timeless personality who captivates us beyond the confines of history—one who does not deserve to be forgotten beneath the dust of time. Queen Marie emerges as the very image of national identity, a model of dedication and unrelenting struggle for Romanian values. David Kimel splendidly highlights her contributions during the cholera epidemic of that era.

"After her meeting with King Carol, Marie returned to Bucharest. She was glad that the sovereign hadn't rejected her request to care for the sick, but at the same time, she knew a great responsibility now rested on her shoulders."

"Marie continued to visit the sick each day, speaking with them, trying to ease their longing to return to their untended lands […] The people understood and listened to her because they knew her. They had known her since they crossed the Danube, marching over the pontoon bridge where she waited for hours with her arms full of flowers, offering each man a bloom as a gesture of welcome home."

A fine observer, the author portrays the intricacies of society, the state of the nation and the army, the political context, and the complexity of diplomatic maneuvers—all woven into a grand fresco, whose steady balance is sustained by the delicate thread of a love story. This love, blossoming and enduring, gives the book a perfectly rounded arc, leaving the reader with a deep sense of optimism—life goes on.

Starting from real historical events, real people and public figures, and adding carefully imagined fictional characters, David Kimel, through this book, brings a heartfelt tribute to Queen Marie—a gesture of respect and gratitude toward those who came before us. It is a profoundly successful and unconventional lesson in patriotism—a book I recommend to readers of all ages.

Congratulations, Mr. Kimel!

Cristina Constatinescu

Chronicle of a Page of History

The appearance of a novel is usually closely linked to the way in which the author lays out their intentions to be as fully understood as possible by readers who love the genre. In this beautiful, engaging, and captivating novel, *Domniţa and Tudor Avădanei*, Mr. David Kimel undertakes a true immersion into the often-turbulent history of Romania at the end of the 19th century and the beginning of the 20th.

What is particularly impressive is the volume of historical documentation the author has researched, highlighting the decisive events that Romania faced, including important aspects of how relations with neighboring countries were managed. True to his style, which often focuses on key historical figures, the author pursues this direction by weaving together deeply human emotions—love, admiration, respect, and esteem—into a delicate and unspoken romantic connection between Princess Marie and the schoolteacher Tudor Avădanei, a relationship which later blossoms into a family through Mura, the Princess's loyal maid, and Tudor. The meeting of these characters in a natural setting propels the novel's plot forward, and their emotional delicacy seems contagious, subtly influencing the behavior of those around them.

The bright side of daily life for Romanian inhabitants is

abruptly disrupted by a momentous event—the Balkan War—with all its devastating consequences, made worse by a lethal, highly contagious disease: cholera, which at the time was difficult to control, despite the efforts and discoveries of Romanian scientists in the medical field. The novel highlights the role of doctors and researchers who strove to contain the spread of the disease through strict hygiene and isolation measures, achieving moderate success.

The author's intention to portray the state of the Romanian army during the war is clear, with a focus on the morale of the soldiers. These descriptions are rendered with remarkable finesse, presenting representative characters endowed with spiritual qualities shaped by innate decency and further refined by family upbringing and education—though not without exceptions.

Mr. Kimel succeeds in composing a rich fresco, a chronicle of a society in full development, revealing his talents as a keen social observer of the era and offering readers the opportunity to reflect on the respective roles of the people and the leaders in shaping history.

His faithful depiction of Romanian society during this period includes an intriguing portrayal of the political practices of the time, as successive governments took power, providing readers with a vivid historical panorama.

Every action of the novel's protagonists is described with care and particular attention to detail, bringing brilliance even to situations that might initially appear uncertain. This can be likened to the extraordinary touch of a painter who, with a single radiant stroke, brings a special painting to life.

This novel, which required immense research and documentation, flows naturally—like a river adapting to the contours of the landscape.

It is a fascinating, absorbing, and enjoyable read, rich in historical significance and depth.

Ionel Gurău

David Kimel's "Domniţa and Tudor Avădanei"

Mr. David Kimel's novel is set against a pivotal period in Romanian history—just before and during the reign of Queen Marie—and it is a dense, well-rooted narrative anchored in the realities of the time. For me, someone who knew little about the governments in power or the various contributions of the prime ministers of that era, the book also served as a valuable source of documentation. Though it is, by genre, a novel, it offers pertinent, precise information, sometimes drawn directly from Queen Marie's own journals (*The Story of My Life*, *War Diary*, etc.). Her Majesty was not only a diplomatic talent and a soldier-queen, but also a remarkable literary voice.

I will not delve into the details of the plot, which is also a love story—making the reading experience both enjoyable and engaging—while painting a vivid fresco of that historical period. It is a book rich in substance and deep insights. Characters like Mura, Tudor, and Izu, along with well-known public figures of the time, give a human dimension to an era that was both heroic and tragic.

The prose is fluent, intelligent, and sensitive, offering deep satisfaction to the reader. It opens not only a window onto that specific period—with all the values and loyalties that defined it—but also a broader view of the world. A time when some hopes and destinies are built, and others crumble, depending on shifting circumstances, or on the way historical winds blow—and, we learn, also about the conscience of those who act. It is a novel that portrays difficult times, filled with sacrifice and renunciation, but also with decisive choices made with a sense of duty, where sovereigns *gave far more than they received.*

It is, I believe, also a testament to the power of transformative decisions that shape history. As Queen Marie herself once remarked:

"Tomorrow may be yours, if your hand is strong enough to seize it."

Milenia Munteanu

Author's Preface

xx

Domniţa şi Tudor Avădanei is a historical novel set in one of the most turbulent periods of modern Romanian history: the years leading up to and during the beginning of the First World War. Romania, a relatively young kingdom, stood at the crossroads of empires — the Austro-Hungarian to the northwest, the Russian to the northeast, and the Ottoman, centuries long legacy still lingering across the Danube River, to the south.

Caught between the rivalries of the Entente and Central Powers, Romania maintained an uneasy neutrality until 1916. The decision to join the war on the side of the Allies came with the hope of uniting all Romanians with Transylvania under one nation — a dream that had long burned in the hearts of its people.

This novel weaves together a fictional love story — that of schoolteacher Tudor Avădanei and the mysterious Mura — with the very real struggles of a nation grappling with identity, loyalty, and sacrifice. It brings to life figures like Queen Marie of Romania, a charismatic and pivotal figure whose influence extended far beyond the palace walls, and Prime Minister Ion I.C. Brătianu, whose political acumen steered Romania through an uncertain time.

The events, while rooted in documented history, are filtered through the emotions and choices of their characters. The settings — from the dusty roads of Copăceni to the heart of Bucharest and the battlefield hospitals — serve as living testimony to a nation's ordeal and resilience.

This story aims to preserve the spirit and authenticity of the Romanian diverse landscape while offering readers a window into the soul of a people at a defining moment in their past. A glossary at the back provides context for Romanian terms and customs that may be unfamiliar.

May this story have the power to reach across borders and times, to move peoples spirit, as does the love of its storyteller.

David Kimel

Domnița and Tudor Avădanei

A Novel

DAVID KIMEL

Life is a Whirlwind

"Life is a whirlwind — a swift and restless river that follows its destined course, carrying us to unforeseen shores, but how could we hope to resist it? What strength do we - mere mortals - possess against waters force given by God in the first moments of Creation? Yes, water is eternal and everlasting. We, people, are but creatures of limited life. Who, then, could ever stand against it?"

Seated at the wheel of an open carriage, driving through the fresh morning air along a rutted country road, Maria turned these thoughts over in her mind because the night before, she had a dream. She had seen herself once more as a young girl in Malta, where her father, Prince Alfred, Duke of Edinburgh, commanded the British naval fleet stationed upon that island in the midst of the Mediterranean Sea. The gardens, the parks, the beaches returned to her with vivid clarity — places where she and her younger sister, Victoria Melita, whom all fondly called Ducky, would race wildly on spirited young colts, as untamed as the girls themselves. Ah, how beautiful those days were! Living in pure freedom, untouched by sorrow or restraint, spent galloping from dawn to dusk as though the whole universe belonged to them. They were the happiest years of her life. Who could have foreseen that such golden days would come to an end — and that everything would change so utterly?

A such familiar sadness came over her, as it always did whenever she recalled the day she had parted, heartbroken, from her family, her sisters, her parents — the day she climbed the steps of the royal carriage sent from Romania by Uncle Karl[i], after her marriage to Nando[ii]. This winter marked twenty years since their farewell.

Life is a whirlwind! Twenty years, six children, and now, at nearly thirty-eight years of age, she scarcely recognized herself. She understood now that she was no longer the girl she once had been, that she had changed, that new experiences had entered her life, reshaping the way she saw both the people and the events of the present and the past, but all these changes had come upon her so swiftly, as if the very days themselves had grown shorter. Back then, she had been but a naive, rather foolish young girl. The whirlwind — this whirlwind of life — in which she had allowed herself to drift, unaware of the consequences, had granted her new eyes and a new measure by which to judge more clearly what had unfolded within her and around her.

The wide plain of ripening fields, shimmering gold beneath the touch of the sun, unfurled before her along the unpaved road she had chosen at random. A shadoof rose slenderly above the tall grain — as high as a grown man — and Maria eased her speed a little, trying to discern her surroundings. Behind her lay the forest from which she had come; to her right, the plain edged by a line of trees and the steeple of a church bell tower, rising sharply against the sky; ahead of her, on the opposite side of the road, stood the well sweeping and a few cattle, chewing their cud with lazy contentment. This morning ride — little more than a whim after a cup of café au lait and a croissant — had drawn her down this road toward the village, guided by curiosity and the simple urge to do something different. She had never been one too shy away from discovering something new. The same impulse had seized her years ago, on the Bistrița River, when she had clambered onto a raft that had drifted close to the riverbank. That happened many, many years ago. This memory made her smile now, for the scene seemed almost comical in hindsight — though at the time, unaware of what might befall her, it had been anything but amusing. Fortunately, Nando and Brătianu[iii] had been quick-witted enough to pull her safely out of her predicament.

In those early years — shortly after she arrived in her new country as the wife of the man destined to become the next King of Romania, Prince Ferdinand — her life was far from joyful or satisfying. At that time, for reasons difficult to understand, Uncle Karl, the King, forbade the young couple, Ferdinand and Maria[iv], from forging friendships with others of their own age within the upper circles of local society. Nor were they permitted to travel without the supervision of one of the King's trusted retainers. It was only later that they came to understand the reason. The royal family was not to display any hint of favoritism toward certain locals, for forming friendships could easily provoke the envy of others. It was dangerous to allow a princely household to become the center of a faction; not only do kings attract flatterers, but so too do those who stand close to the throne. Experience had taught the King that a sovereign hears far too many "truths" from his subjects, and that it is no easy task to discern which among them must be taken into consideration. Yet, during these early years in the country, Maria deeply resented the isolation that had been imposed upon her.

"It was like I was a prisoner; a bird in a cage."

She remembered how hard it was to restrain the revolt she felt against such excessive royal tyranny. Before her arrival in Romania, Ferdinand — Nando, as she affectionately called him, had seen little of his own land, apart from a few of the principal cities visited on official occasions as part of his uncle's entourage. When Maria's growing depression became apparent at court, the King, advised by the Crown Council, decided that the princely couple should be taken to visit some of the monasteries around the capital, which to the young princess, these visits held a special charm, both through the simplicity of the monks' way of life and the beauty of the liturgical ceremonies she attended.

Ioan Kalinderu[v], one of Uncle Karl's closest advisors and

entrusted by the King with the administration of the Royal Domains, often acted as the monarch's spokesman when displeasure arose over the conduct of one or both young princes. Seeking to soften the King's rebukes, Kalinderu suggested that perhaps a small excursion for the young couple to some of the Crown Domains along the Bistrița Valley, in Moldavia, might do no harm. As the King raised no objection, the proper arrangements were made, and Ferdinand and Maria set out to visit those lands of which they had heard so much — lands said to be of striking beauty.

Accompanied by Kalinderu and Ionel Brătianu — at that time a man full of good cheer and optimism, not yet forty years old, son of the late Prime Minister Ion C. Brătianu[vi], and formerly the leader of the Liberal Party — they set off on their journey. They camped at one of the houses on the royal domain, decorated according to Kalinderu's not-so-refined taste, adorned with photographs and engravings of the royal family — but above all, with an abundance of photographs of Ion Kalinderu himself: Kalinderu on horseback, Kalinderu at the hunt, Kalinderu at the harvest, and many other images featuring the same central figure.

In the days that followed, traveling in country carriages or sometimes on horseback, they covered many miles along dusty roads and mountain paths, through forests and hills. One afternoon, they made a stop on the banks of the Bistrița River, in the cool shade of a clearing. Maria, gazing at the flowing waters, removed her shoes and dipped her foot into the icy mountain river — only to pull it back at once with a cry. Nando laughed behind her, reminding her that she had been warned. The water was not only cold, but swift as well. A few tiny silver fish darted near the shore in the crystal-clear water, through which the grey riverbed, strewn with mountain stones, could be seen as if through a lens of polished glass.

From upriver, a long raft with several sections came drifting toward them, steered by a burly man who maneuvered it using a long pole pivoted at the center. At a bend in the river, driven by the strong current, the raft crashed into the bank, which had been reinforced with heavy beams lying along the bend of the river, causing the raft to shift direction and follow the new course of the water. Standing just a step away from the edge, Maria impulsively leapt onto one of the trailing sections of the raft. Taken by surprise, Nando jumped angrily after her, and in an instant, they both became unwilling travelers atop the striped logs gliding along the surface of the river. Someone on the shore, seeing the princely couple drifting away on the raft, rushed to the carriage stationed at the edge of the road and, whipping the horses into a gallop, set off in pursuit along the riverbank. Maria, who had never seen a raft before, had no idea that once set adrift, it could not simply stop at will.

"What are you doing?" Nando called out angrily. "It won't stop! We have to jump into the water!"

"What do you mean it won't stop? Why not?" Maria asked, alarmed.

"It only stops at Vatra Dornei, at the lumber mill. We must jump!"

Meanwhile, Ionel Brătianu was racing after them on land, signaling that he was following their course. Maria, seized by fear, hesitated, unsure how she could possibly jump, fully dressed, into that swift, icy, deep water. At another bend, the raft struck the bank again, and Nando and Maria seized the opportunity to leap back onto the stony shore. Nando could barely contain his fury at having been dragged into such a childish escapade.

"How could you do something like that? Why didn't you tell me what you were about to do?"

"I didn't know!" Maria said breathlessly. "It was an instinct... an experience..."

"An experience that could have cost you dearly! Not just you — both of us!"

"I know..." she whispered.

"Now Uncle will hear of it, and he'll be furious all over again," Nando added, troubled.

Thank God, all had ended well. Nando knew that Ionel Brătianu would not breathe a word of this incident, but when it came to old Kalinderu, he was less sure. When the chance came, he pulled Kalinderu aside and said:

"I believe you'll agree with me that there's no need to give His Majesty another reason for concern by informing him about today's little misadventure on the raft..."

"Absolutely!" the old courtier replied. "But I can't promise to deny it if someone else brings it to His Majesty's attention." In Kalinderu's glance, Ferdinand thought he detected a gleam of sly amusement, and he immediately regretted opening the subject.

In gratitude for Maria's thanks, Brătianu promised to organize a proper rafting excursion on the Bistrița before they left those picturesque lands. And not only that — in the days that followed, they also visited the monasteries of Agapia, Văratec, Bistrița, and Neamț, even spending a night at one of them, where the atmosphere of bygone times still lingered. Everywhere they went, they were greeted with flowers, cheers, crowds of people from nearby villages, lavishing feasts, and the joyful ringing of bells that announced the arrival of their distinguished guests.

"Yes, that raft ride was a unique experience!" Maria thought. A whirlwind — just like life itself. When you're caught up in its currents, you can no longer resist. You become like the raft itself, a scrap of wood carried from place to place by the waters, powerless to fight back.

The Heiress of Conu' Filipescu

Bent over a grave, pulling the weeds that had sprung up around the cross, a man noticed the shadow of someone standing behind him. He lifted his head and saw a young woman. Seeing that he had noticed her, she spoke:

"Good day to you."

"And may good be your heart, domniță," he replied.

"Who is buried here?" she asked gently.

"My wife and child... My wife died giving birth, and the child with her..."

"I'm so very sorry. What a heavy loss... When did this happen?"

"Well, it's been about eight years now..."

"Eight years? That long? Did you ever rebuild your life after that sorrow?"

"No, domniță, I couldn't. I never found anyone who could be to me what she was. When Father Pârvu, her father, gave her to me, she had just turned seventeen. And besides, I couldn't — it would have brought sorrow into the priest's household."

"Seventeen? So young?" the lady murmured. She gazed

thoughtfully at the stone cross at the head of the grave, her mind far away. She, too, had been just seventeen when she married — still a child, knowing nothing of life. Why do people allow such marriages, she wondered, before giving children the chance to discover life? There should be a law to forbid such things, she thought, because at that tender age, girls still love to play with dolls.

"Yes, domniță! Seventeen she was!" the man said. "And you, also, have someone buried here?"

"Me? No! I'm only visiting. I like to wander among the graves, to look at the monuments. I stop at some of them, read the inscriptions on the crosses, and sometimes, I even say a prayer for the souls resting there."

"You're not from around these parts, I reckon," he said, studying her.

"That's true. I come from the city. I try to escape the stifling heat of Bucharest. Here, it's cooler, quieter. I love these places. I've recently inherited something nearby, so I'll be visiting more often."

The man stood up, removing his hat, and brushed the dust from his trousers. On the other side of the grave stood the lady — a woman with naturally wavy golden hair, a soft curl falling across her forehead. Her blue eyes were shaded by the brim of a hat through which the sunlight filtered gently. Her skin was fair, as velvety as a ripening peach in summer. She was tall, slender, dressed in a thin white gown as delicate as silk gauze, embroidered with shimmering threads of silk. The man bent down again, plucked a fragile white flower — still beaded with morning dew — and offered it to her.

"From Vasilica and me," he said.

"Thank you," she replied, touched.

"Is your inheritance here, in our village?"

"Close by. It's on the other side of the woods."

"Ah... the manor of the old marshal at the palace? I remember he was quite elderly, poor soul. Perhaps he's passed away by now... Boier Filipescu..."

"Yes. I inherited it from him. His name was Gheorghe Emanoil Filipescu, former Marshal of the Royal Court."

"I knew him. He came around here rarely, especially after his wife passed...The manor was beautiful once, but I reckon it's fallen into disrepair. It'll take some work to bring it back to how it was."

"Indeed. I've brought workers from Bucharest to help. There's still much to do... but perhaps later, when peace comes again..."

"You believe there's going to be war?"

"Isn't there already war everywhere? The Serbs and the

Bulgarians, Greeks and Turks. They are all fighting What do the people in the village think?"

"What do they think? Well, each has their own worries," said the man. "Some have already been called up to the army. Folks my age wonder who's going to harvest the crops this year — it's a good harvest, too. Who's going to plant the fields for the fall? Who's going to look after the children, the animals, and everything else? The older folks grumble that the Russians and Austrians took Bessarabia and Bukovina from us. Father Pârvu says the world has turned wicked, and that's why the Lord sends us lessons — to bring us back to the holy ways."

"Perhaps Father Pârvu is right," the woman said thoughtfully, watching her wristwatch. "But now I must go. I'll come back another time. Farewell to you!"

"Domniță!" the man called after her. "Will you tell me your name?"

"Maria," she answered.

"I'm Tudor, the schoolmaster here in the village. Everyone knows me. Maybe we'll meet again!"

"Maybe," Maria said with a smile as she walked away.

Tudor remained standing, watching her graceful figure as she moved between the rows of graves, heading toward the edge of the cemetery and the road beyond. Passing through the arched gate with a canopy of woven branches over carved wooden doors, she made her way toward the far side of the village road, where a car was waiting with its top left down. Maria climbed into the driver's seat, turned the vehicle around, and set off toward the woods, into the heart of the grove where the old manor she had inherited lay hidden.

Placing his hat back on his head, Tudor turned toward the village. In front of the church, Father Pârvu was talking with a few villagers:

"What brings you here, son?" the old priest asked.

"Nothing in particular, Father. I was coming back from the cemetery. A lady from the city was asking about the grave where Vasilica rests. She said she's the heir to Conu' Filipescu..."

"God rest his soul, he was a good man," said the priest, crossing himself. "And tell me, did you find out who she is?"

"Not really. She only told me her name was Maria..."

"That's not much to go on..." Father Pârvu mused. "I thought the old boy had a nephew who worked for the newspapers, a big man in politics?"

"Wouldn't that be Nică Filipescu, from *Epoca*?" offered Mr. Popescu, the notary from Copăceni.

"But wait — wasn't he the mayor of the capital some years ago?" chimed in old man Zaharia, the wholesaler who ran the village shop.

"No, nene! That was a while back. Just last year, he was Minister of War," the notary corrected him. "Don't you remember? The Conservatives were in power then, with Petrică Carp leading them."

"Even so, we still don't know who inherited Conu' Filipescu's estate," Father Pârvu concluded. The men fell into thoughtful silence.

Tudor lingered a bit longer, chatting with them by the church steps. When he finally made his way home, he hadn't even stepped fully into the yard when his Aunt Ileana, his mother's sister, rushed out to meet him with a letter in her hand.

"Tudor, my boy, look what came for you today! Pamfil, the postman, says you've been called up to the army!"

Embers of Love

In the sweltering afternoons of Bucharest, Prince Ferdinand and his wife, Maria, would sometimes take the car and set off for a drive around the city's outskirts. They were always looking for new routes, even if it meant speeding along dusty, unpaved country roads, where they would pass peasants' carts pulled aside to prevent the animals from being frightened.

One day, they found themselves heading toward Giurgiu, where they entered a shaded forest filled with ancient, thick trees that seemed to invite travelers into their depths. Deeper within, they discovered a manor house — built in the old style and seemingly abandoned by fate. It stood in a clearing among the centuries-old trees, casting a mysterious, almost fairytale-like atmosphere. Although neglected, the place had a certain charm; a serene detachment from the troubles of the world seemed to linger there.

Whenever they had no other plans, the princes made a habit of traveling this way more frequently, not far from the village of Copăceni. In time, they learned the estate belonged to the elderly uncle of Nicolae Filipescu[vii], the Grand Marshal of the Royal Court, George Emanoil Filipescu.

When the old general learned that the Crown Prince and

Princess often visited his place, he was deeply moved, and through his will, he left the entire property to Princess Maria. This gift brought Maria immense joy since she had never possessed something that belonged entirely to her. Passionate and full of energy, as always, she immediately set about transforming the place to her liking — just as she had done years earlier when Uncle Karl, the King, built the Cotroceni Palace for the young heirs to the throne.

When she came to her new country, Maria fell in love with the personality of Romanian style and its simplicity that contrasted so much with the heaviness and elaborated dark forms that crowd other palates. So, a free spirit who loved wide-open spaces and simplicity, Maria replaced the heavy, ornament-laden Baroque furniture — the kind her uncle had crammed into their apartments at the Royal Palace on Calea Victoriei, where she first lived— with a style where practicality was perfectly blended with her liberated spirit. Just as she had at Cotroceni, choosing simple yet functional Brâncovenesc-style furnishings to express herself, so too at this manor did she fill every corner with simplicity — and flowers, abundant flowers bursting with freshness.

Ferdinand, who enjoyed driving the car himself as a way of relaxing, was usually quiet, reserved, thoughtful, and attentive to his wife, though not very talkative. He kept his eyes fixed on the road ahead, carefully steering around potholes and the occasional poultry still unfamiliar with the rules of the highway.

Maria, understanding his need for reflection, refrained from disturbing him with questions or idle suggestions. No, Nando hadn't always been this way. After two decades of marriage and six children, of which the youngest, Mircea, was born earlier that year in January 1913, Maria had come to better understand what had happened between them during this time. The change in his nature, perhaps in hers too, had come slowly, imperceptibly, yet unmistakably, leaving clear traces. Nando had become more silent, more withdrawn, more absent. Perhaps she, too, was no longer the girl she once had been. They had grown, evolved differently — like two branches springing from the same trunk yet stretching away in separate directions, still drawing life from the same sap.

"Could it be that I had contributed to this distance?" she asked herself. Or maybe it would never have happened if Nando, older and more experienced, had tried to guide me, to tell me, make me understand him, and meet needs he had. But he never fully confessed."

Maria knew, before her had been another woman — Elena Văcărescu[viii], whom he had once loved so deeply before they had even met — he might have found greater happiness. But that marriage had been impossible, because the laws forbade members of the royal family from marrying their own subjects.

Nando had always been, in his own way, a sober, quiet,

timid, and reserved man, especially in social circles. He possessed a rich culture, with a broad knowledge that extended into many fields, such as literature, philosophy, history, and science. Flowers had always held a special fascination for him — their beauty and delicacy captivated him — and he developed a true passion for studying and cultivating them, becoming a veritable expert in botany. He could converse fluently in many foreign languages, including Romanian, and being always well-informed, he preferred to remain silent, choosing rather to be thought naive than to appear superior in front of those who, with loud voices, would dive into discussions about things they knew little of. With his characteristic delicacy, Nando tried to shield them, for he would have felt uncomfortable correcting their mistakes.

At the same time, he was shy, and out of fear of making a rash decision, he often chose to remain passive. Lacking self-confidence, he allowed himself to be dominated by others. He had an exceptional intelligence, capable of perceiving the deeper layers of the issues around him, even those carefully concealed, but without the will to act, he was paralyzed by doubt. Maria came, gradually and late, to understand all these traits and flaws of her husband.

"But in the beginning, there was so much love! How much Nando loved me in those days," she thought. "And I, who never knew what love was, I felt so intensely that incredible attraction to him, my only moral support in a world so strange and different from mine."

When Nando first met Missy — the familiar name by which Maria was known among friends and acquaintances — he was immediately captivated by her beauty, freshness, and the spontaneous charm of a sixteen-year-old girl. She was full of that youthful exuberance that only a life lived freely, close to nature, can bestow on those endowed with boundless energy and an effervescent spirit, like the bubbles in a glass of champagne. Her unrestrained playfulness almost caused Nando anxiety whenever Maria, together with her younger sister Ducky, would launch into races at full gallop atop proud Arabian horses with flowing manes and bushy tails. Until then, Maria had paid little attention to men and was surprised when their mother, the Grand Duchess Maria Alexandrovna,[ix] brought them both elegant new dresses, like those worn by the leading ladies on the opera stage. Up to that moment, Missy still felt like a mere child, only just beginning to step into the world.

Ferdinand was a tall, handsome young man, splendid in his military uniform, with a blond mustache and eyes filled with tender understanding.

Their first meeting took place in 1891, at Wilhelmshöhe, near Kassel, an eighteenth-century castle in Germany where Emperor Wilhelm II[x] — who, incidentally, was Maria's cousin — had invited guests during the annual military maneuvers. Maria had been invited there along with Ducky and their mother, the Duchess Maria Alexandrovna.

At the grand court luncheon, when Maria appeared in her gala gown, chosen by her mother, she noticed in one of the imperial vases some orchids that perfectly matched the color of her dress. With her irrepressible ingenuity, she joyfully plucked the orchids from the vase and pinned them to the shoulder of her dress with a hairpin, proud of this new adornment that harmonized so perfectly. Even when she saw her mother's disapproving glance at her addition to the dress, it had not perturbed her very much.

By chance, her seat at the table was next to the Prince of Romania. Both Ducky and she liked this modest, unpretentious young man who tried to win them over, answering each of her questions or comments with an open smile, doing his best to hide his shyness. He was troubled by the fact that he wasn't sure if he properly conversed with her in her native English, but he expressed great joy at being back in Germany, his homeland. Maria wanted to ask him something about his distant country, Romania, but since she didn't exactly know where it was on the map, she blushed and remained silent.

Their second meeting took place the following spring, in Munich, when the duchess came with her older daughters to visit the city, tour the museums, shops, and attend plays and operas. The fact that she ran into Prince Ferdinand again fascinated Maria. Seeing him again was a surprise — this young man with clear sensitivity, a painful timidity, and above all, a visible restraint in any spontaneous action. She sensed that he had an obvious hunger for real experience, but all his eagerness languished without someone to inspire him.

"He had the desire to conquer the stars, if only he'd have wings!" remembered Maria, thinking of Nando. "But he was adorable like that."

Still, a small, surprising event caused Maria to slightly change the way she saw Nando. One pleasant afternoon, he came to take Maria for a walk through the Hofgarten — a garden in the city center that has a pavilion at its heart dedicated to the goddess Diana. After admiring the murals depicting scenes from Bavarian history, they entered the central octagonal pavilion, with eight arches, each opening onto paths leading into the park. Seeing that no one else was around, Ferdinand stopped in front of Maria and tried to kiss her on the lips. Frightened, she pulled away from his embrace and turned her back to him. Nando was taken aback and upset — mostly with himself — and said nothing. Maria asked him to take her home, and they walked the distance in silence. Once home, Maria refused to speak to anyone, not even to the Duchess, who wanted to know what had happened.

The Duchess learned the whole story in detail from her

cousin Charly, Princess of Saxe-Meiningen and sister to Kaiser Wilhelm II. That prompted the duchess to have a talk with her daughters, explaining that it was normal for young admirers to request a kiss — that it was a sign of admiration for a girl, and if she accepted the kiss, it meant the affection was mutual. Refusing a kiss, on the other hand, clearly showed she had no intention of continuing a friendship with that young man. The same cousin, Charly — whom Maria admired for her beauty, elegance, and intelligence — also conveyed to Ferdinand that the situation had been a misunderstanding, that Maria had never had any admirers before him, and that nothing had changed between them.

A new surprise came in May, at the Neues Palais in Potsdam, where, during a banquet, the engagement of Maria and Ferdinand was officially announced — under the jovial gaze of Kaiser Wilhelm II, his wife Augusta Victoria, and several courtiers.

Ferdinand arrived accompanied by his aide-de-camp, Colonel Coandă. He impressed Maria by describing the beauty of Romania, the people who had only recently gained their independence from the Ottomans — a hardworking and peaceful people who eagerly awaited the arrival of their new princess. He told her that preparations were already underway to welcome her there. All of this was conveyed in poetic images that delighted Maria.

More than that, she was delighted seeing Ferdinand radiating so much love — his eyes lit up around her, and the joy he felt whenever they were together was infectious. Even his shy smile, which masked his awkwardness when answering a question, had a special charm. And the way his gaze followed her at every moment left a strong impression on Maria — these were tokens of love she had never imagined possible. She felt that she loved him just as deeply, with the only difference being the sorrow she felt at the thought of leaving her younger sisters, her family, and the places she held so dear.

In the days leading up to their wedding, Maria — accompanied by her mother, the duchess — traveled to Sigmaringen to meet the family of her future husband. Feverish preparations were underway there for the arrival of the Kaiser and King Carol I of Romania. The king, however, did not come with his wife, Queen Elisabeth[xi] , about whom it was rumored that she was in exile. Maria would later learn what had happened two years earlier, when the king had been forced to remove the queen from court to avoid a public scandal.

Queen Elisabeth, also known as the poet queen Carmen Sylva, was driven by an uncontrollable urge to elevate herself as a protector of romantic sentiment. Having brought Prince Ferdinand — the second son of Leopold and brother of King Carol — to Romania as heir to the throne, Carmen Sylva, still grieving the 1874 death of her only daughter, Maria, who had died of typhoid fever at the age of four, poured all her love onto her nephew from Germany. Knowing they could have no more children, King Carol agreed to the proposal of the Liberal Prime Minister I.C. Brătianu to include in the country's constitution a very important provision:

"No member of the royal family is allowed to marry a Romanian subject!"

Even though Queen Elisabeth was aware of this law, she could not help but encourage the romance between Prince Ferdinand and her protégée, Elena Văcărescu, whom she believed to be a reincarnation of her own lost daughter. When Ferdinand approached King Carol to ask for his consent to marry the young woman, the king flew into a rage and immediately exiled Elena Văcărescu to France. The news spread quickly, and to quell public outcry, the king sent the queen back to New Wied, in Germany, to her family. Heartbroken, Carmen Sylva fell ill. Her condition gradually worsened until she could no longer move about except in a wheelchair.

At Sigmaringen, it was in many ways a second engagement for the young lovers — one that included the entire family, with receptions, lavish meals, gifts, and heartfelt wishes. During a formal banquet, King Carol raised his glass and when all discussion ended, he proposed a toast in honor of the young couple:

"I drink to this honey-day celebration!"

Prince Ferdinand drained his glass, but the smile with which he had greeted the previous speakers vanished from his face. Pale with unease, he sat back down, took Maria's hand on his own, and asked her[xii]:

"Did you hear what he said?"

"What was it?"

"He said, 'honey-*day, not honeymoon.*'"

"So what?"

"Don't you get it? He meant we'll only get one *day* of honeymoon, instead of an entire month! That's how he is. He doesn't believe in honeymoons. He's not like everyone else. For him, everything is duty — no room for even a single error — and he expects the whole world to be the same."

Maria didn't give much importance to Ferdinand's comment at the time. But she would soon understand that Nando hadn't exaggerated it. He had spoken the honest truth about the king.

Together with the duchess, Maria later visited Queen Elisabeth in her woodland refuge, where she was living with her mother in a large, isolated house nestled deep within the forest. Many needy locals, impoverished nobles, and distant family members came to her there seeking help.

From their meeting, one moment stood out vividly in

Maria's mind. She had been intimidated from the beginning by the beauty of this woman, whose fame as an illustrious poet had long been known to her. Her talent, education, refinement — and most of all, the way she created a magical atmosphere for that first meeting — left Maria stunned. Like something from a Wagnerian vision, the queen, defeated by illness, had managed to continue her artistic work even from her sickbed, painting for posterity while locked in battle with her own suffering. Deeply moved, Maria pitied both the fate and the injustice that had befallen the poet queen. Yet she would later come to understand that Carmen Sylva had a lifelong tendency to dramatize reality.

Meanwhile, in London, preparations were underway to give King Carol of Romania an exceptional reception. He was greeted with full honors by the entire British royal court and decorated with the Order of the Garter — the highest chivalric order in the United Kingdom, limited to just 24 companions, including Queen Victoria herself and the Prince of Wales.

The ceremony took place on June 30, 1892, in the great oval vestibule of Windsor Castle, where the entire court had gathered — the very place where Queen Victoria, the dear grandmother, loved to receive her guests. The queen's entrance — heralded by the deep thud of her cane striking the stone floor and the rustle of her long black silk gown — was met with bows and curtsies from all present. Small in stature, smiling gently, and shy, she returned each greeting with kindness. When she stopped in front of the even shyer Prince Ferdinand — this being their first meeting for the occasion — she addressed him in German, his native language, her voice graceful and melodic:

"How are your parents, whom I love so dearly?"

"Thank you! They are well."

"I keep a portrait of your mother in my room," the queen added. "She was a marvel of beauty! A true wonder!"

Maria suddenly remembered the painting in her grandmother's room — a portrait of a stunningly beautiful woman resting on an easel — and only now realized that it was a depiction of Nando's mother.

During that visit, the King of Romania had the opportunity to meet privately with Queen Victoria, the most significant historical figure of her era. Queen of Great Britain since 1837 and Empress of India since 1876, by the time of Maria and Nando's wedding in 1893, this delicate woman was sovereign of the most powerful empire in the world and commanded the respect and admiration of all nations.

True to his ever-restless sense of duty — which had never left him — the Romanian king used the few days spent in England to meet with prominent figures in industry, finance, and politics. He visited many institutions, made valuable and necessary contacts at the Bank of England, the Royal Mint, the port docks, and many more.

He also insisted that Ferdinand do the same, but the prince was far too in love during those days to follow his example. The Duchess, though delighted to see her daughter's suitor so clearly enamored, couldn't understand why love and duty were seen as incompatible.

For Maria, the prince's fiancée and her sisters, King Carol had brought beautiful national costumes from Romania, embroidered with silk thread. The girls, delighted by their beauty, hurried off to try them on and soon returned dressed like true Romanian peasant girls — wearing headscarves, belts, embroidered blouses, and vibrant woven skirts, all gleaming with lively colors. Those presents were treated to a first glimpse of the picturesque people from the foothills of the Carpathians, and of the distant country that Missy would soon call home.

The wedding took place in Sigmaringen, a small town in the southeastern region of Germany — Baden-Württemberg — overshadowed by a medieval castle with many levels and defensive towers, built atop a hill around which the Danube River wound its way. At that point, the Danube seemed more like a stream — the same river that would flow across the continent eastward, caressing numerous lands with its gentle waters, offering them wealth borne by the current, connections to distant places, and genuine prosperity. As its waters traveled onward, the river curved as if to embrace the small, mysterious country that Maria would one day rule — a land of golden grain fields in the Bărăgan Plain, shielded from northern winds by the rocky peaks of the Carpathians. At the mountains' feet, the crown of rust-colored forests echoed the murmuring song of springs eager to join the blue river. There, fate rushed to receive Maria — to usher in the birth of a new dynasty.

Sigmaringen Castle, home of the Hohenzollern dynasty — which had given Germany many rulers and emperors since the beginning of the first millennium — had its proud roots as a centuries-old feudal fortress in the Swabian Jura, towering over the town below. In that enchanting setting, Maria was warmly welcomed by every member of Ferdinand's large family and by King Carol, who had arrived with a sizeable entourage of Romania's most prominent government officials.

And then, the processions continued, with guests arriving from all over Europe to the small town, now dressed in its festive finest. Crowds lined the roads, cheering with bouquets of flowers and flags waving in the wind. Among them were Prince Arthur of Connaught, representing England (as Queen Victoria could no longer travel), Wilhelm II, Emperor of Germany, Grand Duke Alexis — brother of the Duchess — sent by the Tsar, and the

Countess of Flanders, King Carol's sister, who came from Belgium with her son, Albert.

It was said that among the entire Hohenzollern family, only the Countess of Flanders and King Carol of Romania shared the same austere nature — equally rigid and flawless in their devotion to duty, leaving no room for diversion toward pleasures, amusements, or comfort.

There were three ceremonies: the civil one, the Catholic ceremony for Ferdinand's faith, and the Protestant one for Maria. It all took place on the same morning. The Catholic ceremony was held in a church within the fortress, featuring a solemn service, choral music, and many clergy. The Protestant ceremony was conducted in one of the palace's grand halls and was officiated by a chaplain from the British Navy, which was still commanded by Maria's father, the Duke of Edinburgh, Alfred.

But when the moment of final farewell with her family drew near, Maria was overwhelmed by a soul-wrenching sorrow. Not even the fact that King Carol had sent a heated royal carriage to bring them into the country, nor the full extent of Nando's love and all his efforts to ease her sadness, could stop the flow of tears that would not cease — and which pained him deeply as well.

"My dear Missy, please don't cry! You'll see — everything will be fine!" Nando tried to comfort her.

"I don't know!... I only know that I feel so alone!... All the people I love, I left behind. I have no one here!"

"I understand — but you're not completely alone. I'm with you!"

"You — you don't understand! I have three sisters and a brother back there. My mother is there, my father, my home!... And they're crying because I left them… You can't be all of them for me… That's why I'm crying. I'm so alone!"

"But you know how much I love you!" Nando insisted, drawing her close to kiss her. "Come — let's just sit here, side by side, and take in the beauty of the places we're passing through."

"No! All of this is foreign to me! Everything you say feels foreign! What do I know about your country?"

"You'll see — it's a country…"

"I know it's a country. But what kind of country? Your silence makes me think it's hell! Is that where you're taking me?"

"It's not hell. But this country is unlike anything you've ever known. It's different — you'll see…"

The journey to the new country continued for several days, passing through lands blanketed in white snow, covering everything — rooftops, trees, valleys, and mountains. The young couple's solitude in the elegant carriage, upholstered in red plush with matching curtains, was accompanied only by the rhythmic ticking of the wheels, beating over the joints in the railway tracks in sync with the ticking of the wall clock.

They entered Romania through Predeal, a border town at the time. While Maria could not tear herself away from the view of the mountains rolling past along Prahova Valley, Ferdinand came to embrace her once more, knowing that the dream of being alone with his beloved was coming to an end. Soon, they would step into the watchful gaze of the public awaiting them. Only in the late hours of the night would they again be together, alone, free to speak and enjoy one another.

"Missy, it's time to get dressed! We'll be there in half an hour," Nando told her gently, kissing her once more.

"Yes, at the beginning, there was love," Maria thought from her seat in the car driven by Nando. "A love so deep it blurred all other feelings — a love that defies words, revealed through our eyes only, pouring like a cascade - constant and full - filling all emptiness."

Such love did exist, for several years, until the slander and false rumors spread by some at court began to poison their lives. These lies robbed them of the right to decide what was best for their children's upbringing. Unable to bear Nando's lack of a firm response and opposition to these humiliating situations, Maria grew distant from him in spirit. The once-consuming blaze of their passion had collapsed into a heap of embers, from which only a few smoldering coals remained — just enough to remind them of the love that had once been.

Flowers on the Grave

In the village, talk of war was becoming increasingly frequent, but only when the draft orders began arriving did people start to show real concern.

"War? God forbids!... Who are we fighting now?" some asked in confusion.

After Sunday service at the church, Tudor went to the cemetery, as he usually did. There, in front of the grave, he felt a sense of peace. His thoughts would unwind more easily, clearer somehow, as if the answers came from somewhere unknown to him, perhaps from Vasilica, his wife, with whom he spoke as if she were right there beside him. He felt bound to her, to the one who had always inspired love in him, and it seemed that by coming to the grave, he could hear her voice again, comforting him. He could still feel the warmth of her spirit, and the grave where Vasilica now rested no longer felt like a place of separation, but rather a link between worlds and times.

When he reached the grave, Tudor found, at the foot of the cross, a bouquet of fresh flowers tied with a wide silk ribbon.

"Who brought these flowers here?" he asked himself.

After mentally going through everyone who might have

done such a thing, he concluded that it could only have been Maria — that stranger with the appearance of a fairy. Ever since he had met her, the image of her — unnaturally pale skin, blonde hair, and eyes shaded by the brim of her hat — had continued to linger in his mind.

"Could these flowers be from her? If not her, then who?"

After lunch at Father Pârvu's house — his father-in-law, who still considered Tudor part of the family — he thought to stop by his own house and find something suitable to bring Maria, as a thank-you for her gesture.

"What's with you, son? You seem more pensive than usual today," the priest asked.

"Nothing in particular, Father. It's just that I found a bouquet of fresh flowers on Vasilica's grave today… and I have no idea who left them."

"Maybe they were left there by mistake. Perhaps they were meant for someone else, but the person changed their mind and left them with Vasilica instead."

"No, because — you see — these aren't wildflowers like the ones that grow around here. And the bouquet is tied with a wide silk ribbon."

"You don't say?" the priest replied, surprised. "Then who

left them?”

“I don’t know! I think it might be that lady I told you about the other day in front of the church. You remember — the one who inherited from old Filipescu… I think they’re from her.”

“Strange,” said the priest, falling into thought.

He took his tobacco case out of the pocket of his cassock, which was tied at the waist with a wide sash, and rolled himself a cigarette. Then Tudor set off for his house. On the way, he thought he might take a detour past the former boyar’s manor, maybe he’d catch another glimpse of Maria.

Once home, he took off his jacket and the necktie—too warm outside for such attire on a walk to the estate. Then he looked around for something more presentable, something he could bring as a gift for Maria, something she might like.

Glancing about, his eyes fell on a thick book lying on the table. Between its pages, he found a pressed rose, still holding the bright red hue of its petals.

“Maybe this?” he wondered to himself. “No, that’s not enough. I need to add something more.”

He took a school notebook from a shelf and sat down at the table. He opened it, tore out a page from the middle, picked up a pencil, and sat still for a moment, eyes resting on a vase of flowers in the center of the table, wondering what he should write. After a while, he set the first words down on the page:

Among the graves where silence sighs,

The wind alone in mourning flies,

And I, who have no home to share,

Still dream that my bride waits me there.

For she has gone to God above,

And left me lost without her love.

Since then, I roam without a goal,

As if her grave had claimed my soul.

Each dusk I sigh beneath the skies,

Where clouds like sorrow slowly rise,

Still aching with a burning grief —

For fate has never brought relief.

Here, Tudor stopped writing:

"Is what I wrote really true?" he wondered. "After eight years, what could be truer than this? It's as if the world around me stopped turning the moment Vasilica died. It's as if I died along with her. The only difference is—I haven't been buried yet."

Then he remembered the army draft notice he received the other morning:

"That's where fate's taking care of it. That's why I'm going to war," Tudor told himself.

He gripped the pencil in his hand and began to write again:

Then Heaven's Lord, in mercy mild,

Did call upon His cherished child,

And summoned swift an angel fair,

To be my guide through the day's despair.

An angel robbed in shining white,

With golden hair and eyes of light,

Whose voice flowed soft like streams at play,

And gently to my heart did say:

DOMNIȚA AND TUDOR AVĂDANEI

"Weep no more, O soul weighed down,

Tears alone won't earn a crown.

As heavy clouds drift past the skies,

So, sorrow fades and pain must die.

Now take your pack, you wandering man,

And follow fate's unfolding plan!

Through fields of brave and fearless men,

Were battle calls again, again."

"For now's the time to act and rise,

While thieves and foes defile the skies,

And trample all that's pure and true —

Your faith, your roots, the land you knew!"

So, I took up my pack with haste,

And left the village, I embraced.

A star above, my path to chart,

And that bright angel near my heart.

He read the poem once more, from beginning to end, nodded thoughtfully in approval, then set about copying it neatly in ink, just like children do at school. He placed the pressed flower inside a folded sheet of white paper, on which he wrote: "I pressed this rose as a keepsake, on the day I met you." Then he carefully folded the edges of the sheet around the flower and, finding an envelope, wrote on it: "For Maria." He slipped the flower and the freshly written poem inside and left.

The sun shone gently on his shoulders as he walked along the dusty country road, but Tudor's mind kept replaying the words of the poem, doubting whether they would make a good impression on the distinguished lady from Bucharest. As he approached the shaded area of the ancient forest trees, the cool air caressed his sweat-covered face, and he fumbled in his pockets for a crumpled handkerchief to wipe his brow and neck.

Nestled deep in the woods, the manor of General Filipescu was built in the Brâncovenesc style, with vaulted terraces supported by sturdy columns resting on rectangular bases. A nearby watchtower guarded the property with the same serene reverence as the trees surrounding it. Like so many buildings from the late 19th century, the calm beauty of the whitewashed house, with its red-tiled roof and thick fortress-like walls, gave the impression of timeless permanence, untouched by any outside force.

Walking up the path that led to the manor, holding one corner of the envelope to avoid crushing the flower inside, Tudor scanned through the trees, hoping to spot someone who might tell him something about Maria. The alley brought him to the front of the house. After a brief wait, a young woman appeared in the doorway, shaded by a roof supported by two columns. Tudor stepped forward timidly:

"Good afternoon! May I speak with Madam Maria?"

"Madam Maria? What did the person you're looking for look like?"

"Well, as far as I know, she inherited this house…"

"Ah, I see. Please wait here while I go and ask!"

After a short while, the young woman appeared at the edge of the steps and invited him inside. A spacious hall opened before him, with white walls bathed in the afternoon sunlight that streamed through the arched windows. Around the room stood a grand piano, polished to a deep black sheen, a divan covered with cushions wrapped in peasant-style woven fabrics, a carved wooden bench matching the folk motifs of the central table, upon which a vase of fresh flowers brought a lively charm to the space, a tall armchair with carved arms, and high-backed chairs—all painted the same deep brown-black as the piano.

Tudor was invited to take a seat and was told that the lady would be with him shortly. Maria appeared not long after, dressed in a white gown adorned with embroidery.

"Thank you, Mura," Maria said with a smile to the young woman.

Then, turning to Tudor, she asked:

"How are you, Mr. Tudor?"

"Good day, my lady!" said Tudor, rising to his feet as she entered. "This morning, on my way to the cemetery, I found a beautiful bouquet of flowers on my wife's grave. I thought perhaps you had left them there, and I came to thank you."

"It's true—I was there this morning," Maria replied. "I picked a few flowers from my garden and brought them. But please, sit down."

She lifted a small silver bell from the table and rang it softly, the sound lingering in the air.

"Mura, would you mind serving tea here?" she said to the young woman who had let Tudor in.

The girl gave a slight bow and stepped away.

"Very beautiful flowers!" Tudor continued. "I was deeply

touched that you didn't forget my wife's modest grave. I thought I might bring you something in return. I hope you won't take offense at my boldness," he said, handing her the envelope.

"On the contrary—it's a pleasure," said Maria as she opened the envelope. "I'll treasure your gift," she said when she saw the pressed flower. "Ah, but there's more!" she added.

She unfolded the sheet of paper containing Tudor's poem and, after reading it, said:

"Beautiful verses. Truly beautiful. Did you write them yourself?"

"Yes," Tudor replied modestly.

As he conversed with his hostess—this graceful woman, youthful in appearance and refined in manner—Tudor felt his earlier confidence start to waver. He was clearly moved by the warm welcome, the understated elegance of the surroundings, and the natural ease with which she moved, all of which spoke of her noble upbringing. Watching her, Tudor had the strange impression he had seen her somewhere before, though he couldn't place were. The same feeling had stirred in him during their first meeting at the cemetery.

"I've received orders to report for military service," Tudor said. "To tell you the truth, I was expecting this. You see, here in our village, there's a lot of stagnation. Aside from the daily struggles, nothing seems to change. But the world isn't standing still—something is boiling around us, there's a great deal of unrest…"

"We might go to war this year. Aren't you afraid?"

"I don't know. I don't think so. You see, I was born in the year we freed ourselves from the Turks—the year of our Independence. Freedom means a lot to me. My father gave his life for it. If someone comes to take it from us, they'll have to deal with me—and with others like me!"

Just then, Mura arrived carrying a large tray with porcelain cups, teapots, and a platter of assorted pastries. Maria thanked the girl and poured a cup of tea for Tudor, then one for herself.

"Yes, but not everyone is like you," Maria said. "Some doubt we'll succeed. They say we don't have the courage to fight, that they're stronger than us."

"Courage? Didn't we have the courage to crush the Turks at Plevna and Vidin? Haven't all our princes fought and driven out invaders time and again? We have courage because we've always wanted to be free. We've never gone off to conquer other lands—but others have always come to take ours! Even the Romans set their sights on this land, and after them came the barbarians, and one by one, all the rest from around us…But they've gone, and we still are here."

"Yes. That's true," Maria agreed.

Following her gesture, Tudor took the offered teacup and a biscuit from the tray.

"Are you certain we'll go to war?" he asked.

"Yes, I believe so. Soon. It won't be easy. We must be prepared. We need weapons, supplies, hospitals—and time is short. But we'll succeed!"

Tudor fell silent for a moment, deep in thought. During that pause, Maria studied the man seated before her—a man of the people, but more refined. She knew he was a schoolteacher, which meant he had more education than most, and likely read more, too. His face was sun-darkened, his hands calloused, yet clean, his nails neatly trimmed. In his eyes flickered a glint of native intelligence that spoke of determination and vigor.

She had seen the same confident gleam in the eyes of other men she admired—Ionel Brătianu, for instance. Even Barbu Știrbey, who skillfully masked his firmness behind a polished politeness.

"Tudor is an interesting man," Maria thought.

"A great pity!" said Tudor aloud. "The world had just begun to settle down after the great powers decided in London what lands belonged to whom…"

"That's not all," Maria replied. "As you know, the Bulgarians defeated the Ottomans with the help of Serbia and Greece. There should've been peace after that, shouldn't there? But there isn't. Do you know why? Because Bulgaria hasn't had its fill of war. They claim now that Macedonia is theirs—but it's not! That's why the Second Balkan War started. Now they're fighting their former allies, Greece and Serbia."

"And what do they want with us?"

"They want Dobruja back. You see, Mr. Tudor, there are many things in this world that aren't as they should be... In Transylvania, most of the population is Romanian—by language, by dress, by faith. So, wasn't it only natural for Transylvania to be part of Romania? Why isn't it? The same goes for Bessarabia and Bukovina. The great powers took advantage of their might and grabbed what they wanted from the small ones. Now the Bulgarians believe they're the strongest in the region and are making claims on other people's land."

"I understand, but I have a question. We fought the Turks, and rightly so—they bled us dry for centuries, worse than leeches— and I didn't mind seeing them crushed. But these people, Bulgarians, Sărbians and Greeks are Christians, like us... Don't they see it's a sin to kill one another?"

"It is a sin, just as you say! Like brothers fighting over a rickety stool left by their grandmother… What can you do? That's the way of the world! Maybe we won't have to fight them, but they need to see we are strong, and they must fear us".

"We will fight! That's certain—because we've had enough of being oppressed! It's gone on too long! If the enemy doesn't understand that they'll learn we know how to defend our homeland!" said Tudor, a little embarrassed by the fervor in his own voice.

"It's true—we all feel the same," said Maria, reading the emotion in his words.

"You asked me if I'm afraid. I think a soldier doesn't have time for fear. When would he even think about it? He must handle everything on his own: keep watch, look after his comrade, find food, withstand the weather—whether good or bad—and so on. In battle, when bullets are flying past you, if you start thinking about death, you're finished!"

A moment of silence settled between them, after which Maria lifted the little bell from the table and rang it. Soon, Mura entered the salon.

"Mura, do you remember the gift from the abbess at Pasărea Monastery? It should be in the right-hand drawer in my study. Could you bring it to me, please?"

The girl returned shortly, carrying a small box wrapped in dark velvet.

"Mr. Tudor," said Maria, "I believe I have something for you. A talisman to protect you from harm." She paused. "I received this medallion from the abbess at Pasărea Monastery on my last visit."

Tudor, now on his feet, hesitantly opened the box and saw inside a silver medallion, about the size of a fifty-bani coin, hanging from a chain. It depicted the Virgin Mary holding the Infant Jesus.

"My lady… madam… I don't know quite how to say this. We hardly know each other. Thank you, but you shouldn't have! I think you might need it yourself, for protection... These are troubled times, and who knows what lies ahead?"

"You need it more than I do—you're going off to war."

Tudor sat back down, unsure of what to say. He finished his tea, glanced outside where the daylight was starting to fade, set the cup back on the tray, and stood again, signaling it was time to go.

"May the Lord watch over you," he said. "And perhaps I'll have the chance to see you again!"

"Thank you, Mr. Tudor. Your visit was a pleasure. Whether peace or war comes, I hope it all turns out well, and we will meet again. Go safely and take care of yourself. With God's help, all will end well," said Maria, extending her hand in farewell.

"God bless," said Tudor, bending to kiss her hand.

"God bless you, Mr. Tudor."

Maria followed him to the top of the steps and watched him for a while as he made his way down the road toward the village. After returning inside, she called Mura:

"Would you please go and ask His Highness if he would like us to return home tonight?"

High Society

52

As evening approached, a dark blue automobile made its way along the Giurgiu Road toward Bucharest. At the wheel, Prince Ferdinand was trying to shield his eyes from the sunset's glare reflected through the rearview mirror. Adjusting the mirror's angle, he turned his head to glance at Maria, seated beside him in the front seat.

"What are you planning to do tomorrow?" he asked.

"I'm not exactly sure," Maria replied. "Martha Bibescu mentioned wanting to visit the Simu Museum—apparently, they've put up a few new paintings, a Delacroix, and something else I can't remember. Maybe we'll go together."

Ferdinand recalled that three years earlier, he and Maria had been invited to cut the ribbon at the museum's official opening. Built in the heart of the city on Brătianu Boulevard, the Simu Museum had stunned the entire nation with its classical beauty—supported by white marble columns that evoked the grandeur of ancient Greek buildings on the Acropolis.

Resembling temples encircled by Ionic columns, like the Erechtheion dedicated to the goddess Athena, the Simu Museum had quickly earned a reputation as a temple of universal art and culture.

Art lovers entered its halls with the reverence of worshippers entering a cathedral. They were overcome with a sense of awe and joy at the sight of each new object, painting, sculpture, or artifact—each a one-of-a-kind treasure, discovered within the halls of this temple-like institution.

The museum had been envisioned and created by the great boyar and distinguished man of letters, Anastase Simu, who had traveled through the world's foremost cultural centers. Driven by his desire to offer Bucharest something worthy of global civilization, he dedicated the museum to the arts, exhibiting his own personal collection—an extraordinary assemblage of priceless artworks from around the globe. The Simu Museum was continuously enriched with new acquisitions: paintings by great European masters, valuable sculptures, drawings, elegant pieces of furniture, and rare volumes of artistic significance. All these were donated to the country, for Anastase Simu was driven by the ideal: *"Not just for ourselves, but for others as well!"*

During this time, Maria's thoughts turned to the past, a past that had filled her soul with countless days of dissatisfaction and loneliness, with no one close by to confide in, no one to whom she could shed her tears. She felt like a prisoner in this foreign land, bound by unfamiliar laws and customs, from which there was no escape. Young and inexperienced, she had once experienced moments of illusion, such as when she first arrived in Bucharest.

Before the train even came to a stop in the station, it crawled slowly along the crowded platform, filled with cheers and a military brass band. As the train rolled past the brightly lit platform, rows of soldiers and officers from the Mountain Hunters' unit—commanded by Nando—stood aligned along the tracks, cheering over the blare of the military band music. A mass of people surged forward, waving handkerchiefs in the wind, following the train until it reached its stopping point. Another group of dignitaries stood imposingly in the background, dressed in overcoats, black suits, and tall hats, waiting just behind Uncle Karl, by a red carpet rolled out to meet the steps of the royal carriage.

At the top of the steps, Maria was welcomed by her uncle, who stepped forward to help her down from the train. He embraced her warmly, kissing her on both cheeks. The genuine joy in his expression spoke volumes—it was clear to Maria now that his joy sprang from the satisfaction of a long-awaited dream come true. He had finally succeeded in uniting under the Romanian crown the most influential kingdoms of the globe: England, Russia, and Germany. From now on, this tiny country, seemingly insignificant, tucked away on Europe's periphery in 1866, the year of its arrival—had risen from the dust and gained the respect of other nations, especially after winning independence from the Ottomans in 1877. Through Ferdinand's marriage to Maria, a stable dynasty had been secured.

"Who wouldn't be proud of such achievements?" thought Maria, recalling those moments. "Grandma Victoria allowed her son to marry the Russian Tsar's daughter, to secure peace in Europe. She herself married a German prince. But no one marveled at such a grandiose plan like the one Uncle Karl concocted: to wed the strongest forces of the world through my marriage."

After she was introduced to the ministers, generals, high clergy, and judges—all came to greet her, accompanied by their wives dressed in the latest fashions from Parisian journals—the party proceeded to the Metropolitan Orthodox Cathedral for a religious service. There, a solemn *Te Deum* was sung by a large choir. What followed was a procession through the capital's main boulevards in the royal silver carriage with wide glass windows, in the company of King Carol and Prince Ferdinand. Romanian and British flags fluttered in the wind, and people lined the snow-covered roadsides on both sides, hoping to catch even a fleeting glimpse of the princess who had come from afar to be their queen.

When they arrived in front of the Royal Palace, which at that time had only two floors, a sea of people filled the square to greet them, with speeches, the traditional bread and salt, and countless curious eyes pressing forward to catch a glimpse of her.

At that time, the Royal Palace had little to impress a monarch beyond the two sentries posted at the entrance and a frozen fountain in the center of the courtyard. King Carol had made considerable improvements to the old princely palace, originally built by the stolnic Dinicu Golescu, adding new wings in 1881 along with electric lighting, which at the time was still a novelty. The apartment the king had designated for the princely couple was on the upper floor, in the palace's left wing. It consisted of numerous rooms, with many tall doors, heavy drapes over the windows, and walls crowded with paintings. The décor—with its towering ceilings and heavy baroque and rococo furniture in dark tones—instantly disheartened Maria, who felt small and insignificant in its midst. There was nothing living or warm in those rooms to draw close to, no flower to soften the somber atmosphere, which only deepened the ache she felt for home and those she had left behind.

"Is this really to be my new home?" Maria asked herself. She could hardly believe she was expected to spend the rest of her life in that space, which felt more like a warehouse for old furniture waiting to be auctioned than a royal residence. The thought struck her as unbearable.

After her uncle had left them to rest, Nando came closer and embraced Maria[xiii].

"Are you tired?" he asked.

"Yes. A little."

"These dreadful official ceremonies..."

"Yes, they were a bit long..."

"You must rest now, because there's a grand banquet tonight."

"Yes... a grand banquet," she replied, her voice barely above a whisper.

Maria remembered that banquet from the first evening—and all the ones that followed. Endless speeches, full of flattering remarks and best wishes for the young couple, dance invitations from old, overweight men with distorted faces, pinched by the fashionable monocle they wore. Rarely among them was there a more pleasant face with whom she might have had an interesting conversation. Even the officers in attendance werc mostly older men, dressed in glittering formal uniforms, their chests heavy with medals. They all displayed a certain courtly manner, likely carried over from their youth, which they now exhibited as best they could, something that, more than anything, amused Maria.

The ladies, dressed in elegant gowns and wearing sophisticated hairstyles, conversed fluently in the language of Voltaire—some even more fluently than Maria herself. They surrounded her with curiosity, eager to learn how she liked Romania, what impression the welcome had made on her, what she thought of the palace, and other such questions. Embarrassed, she often didn't know what to say to these impromptu interviews, which she found overwhelming and intrusive.

Each day brought a new ball held in her honor, another foreign or provincial delegation presenting gifts. And every night, once the receptions were over, the king and his nephew would withdraw to their apartment to discuss political or military matters until late into the night. Maria began to feel completely drained of energy and strength.

She, who had never known what was to be ill, now found herself feeling unwell. A strange malaise took hold of her. She noticed she was gaining weight, which worried her. With no one she could confide in, she was grateful when her lady-in-waiting, Miss Monson, came to say goodbye before returning to England. But even Monson was perplexed to see her so subdued and dispirited[xiv].

"My dear child, you don't seem very cheerful! Are you feeling all right? You look a bit pale."

"No, I don't feel well at all. I don't know what's happening to me—I get dizzy for no reason, I feel nauseous, and food disgusts me. And I, who never had trouble adjusting to different climates, just can't seem to get used to this one. Everything makes me sick. I don't even recognize myself."

"Well, my dear, that's actually a very good sign! Everyone will be so happy!"

"Happy? Why? Because I'm feeling sick?"

"Oh, sweetheart, surely you know what it means when a young wife starts feeling ill like this?"

"What do you mean?" asked Maria, tears welling in her eyes.

"You don't mean to tell me that no one ever explained this to you?"

"Explain what?" asked Maria, even more confused.

Lady Monson sat beside her and gently explained why the king, the royal family, and the entire country would rejoice at such news.

On the 15th of October 1893, at one o'clock in the morning, Maria gave birth to Carol II. He was the first member of the royal family to be baptized in the Orthodox faith, on the 29th of October 1893, a date that also marked Maria's eighteenth birthday. Before Carol II had even turned one, Maria gave birth to a second child, a daughter, in 1894. The entire nation rejoiced. The country's dynasty was now secure.

But Maria was filled with dread. Under the pretext that her own children belonged to the nation and not to the parents who had brought them into the world, their upbringing was entrusted to educators selected by the king. Queen Elisabeth - the queen-poet Carmen Sylva - who had returned to the country shortly before the birth of the little girl, baptized the child with her own name—Elisabeth.

Returning to the country, the queen did not bring harmony to the royal family that Maria had long hoped for. In her loneliness, she had yearned for the support of a motherly heart, one full of understanding and tenderness. She remembered the state in which she had seen Carmen Sylva back at New Wied palace—sick and suffering, a figure Maria had pitied with all her sincerity. But upon her return to Romania, the queen appeared remarkably lively and in good health. Energetic, authoritative, and imposing as ever—beautiful, dignified, and refined—she was just as admirable as she had been in Germany.

Maria was captivated by the commanding presence of this woman, whose remarkable talent for moving, speaking, and elevating even the most ordinary things never ceased to impress her. Surrounded by her admirers, Carmen Sylva stood in regal majesty, her superb voice enchanting everyone as she recited classical poetry from memory. With her deep culture, she would present new theories on various subjects or fall into moments of poignant nostalgia.

The queen's circle consisted of a few ladies-in-waiting, often joined by guests from the arts—painters, poets, or musicians. Among them, George Enescu -greatest Romanian Musician - was a regular guest in the queen's salon at Peleș Castle every summer. In a tribute article published in *Revista Fundațiilor Regale* (The Journal of Romanian Foundations) in 1943, Enescu recalled[xv]:

"[...] The Queen adopted me in spirit when she returned from Germany after a long absence. My *Poème Roumaine* had been performed in Paris, and Princess Elena Alexandra Bibescu—daughter of the former Prime Minister and head of the Conservative Party, Manolache Costache Iepureanu, the predecessor of Lascar Catargiu—had written to her about me. I was about fifteen at the time and had studied for a year and a half in Paris when Princess Bibescu first heard of me and took me under her protection. When I finished composing the *Poème Roumaine*, she introduced me to Édouard Colonne, who conducted it when I was just sixteen and a half... Upon my return to the country, this activity opened the palace doors for me. King Carol took an interest in me as a hard-working man, and Carmen Sylva in my compositions—she adopted me in spirit, calling herself my second foster mother, knowing that my first had been Princess Bibescu.

I was at Peleș the day the Queen and we all learned of Princess Bibescu's death, at the Iepureanu estate in Moldavia. We remembered her that day by playing string quartets from morning to evening—the Queen, Dinicu, Loebel, and I. It was the summer of 1903. That was how Queen Carmen Sylva understood honoring her beloved and worthy friends—through art".

It was hard to resist the charm of this poet-queen, Carmen Sylva—her culture, refinement, and the captivating charisma with which she had immediately won over Maria. But the Queen's temperament was just as strong and determined as the King's, with the difference that, while King Carol was guided by an acute sense of duty—every move, word, or gesture carefully considered, Queen Elisabeth filtered everything through the lens of her innate romanticism.

She held fast to a blend of religious dogma that, in practice, often showed a narrowness of understanding, mixed with a tendency to heed whispers and rumors, and to make impulsive decisions that frequently caused complications. All of this clashed with Maria's nature. Maria was not used to restraining her emotions, she expressed what she thought directly, without pretense or detours. This candor often gave gossipmongers plenty of fuel to twist her words and actions, attributing to the young princess' behaviors and intentions that did not befit her situation or rank.

Since early childhood, Maria had been accustomed to life in the open air, riding strong horses, delighting in all beautiful things, and savoring an unrestrained sense of freedom. But here, among the provincial mindsets of certain courtiers, all those qualities that animated Maria were seen as flaws. Only her uncle Karl had gradually begun to show a spark of joy at his niece's presence, admiring her courage, her sharp wit, and the firmness with which she defended her dignity.

In the summer of 1896, the princes of Romania were sent to represent their country at the head of a delegation attending the coronation of Tsar Nicholas II in Moscow, following the death of his father, Tsar Alexander III—who was also the brother of Maria's mother, the Duchess. It was on this occasion that Maria truly realized, for the first time, the power of her own beauty and personal charm.

Her cousins on her mother's side—tall, vigorous young men full of vitality and humor—showered her with attention, inviting her to soirées, social events, horseback races on famed Cossack horses, and picnics. Amused by all this attention and by the gallantry of her youthful companions—which annoyed Nando, unaccustomed as he was to such lively gatherings, Maria felt a sort of envy for the dazzling splendor of the tsarist court, so starkly absent at King Carol's austere court.

On the glorious day of the coronation, after the religious ceremony concluded in the Kremlin Cathedral, the Tsar and Tsarina appeared before the public from the heights of the great tower. From there, the crowds gathered from every corner of Russia flooding the city with torrents of love and expectation. Nobody was prepared to witness the horrifying event—a tragedy that would come to foreshadow the sorrowful fate and future suffering of their nation like an unavoidable blasphemy.

"I remember, I cried that day," recalled Maria.

At the end of the day, a grand public celebration was to take place on the Khodynka Field, in honor of the Tsar's coronation. It had been decided that each person attending the festivity would receive a souvenir bearing the likeness of the new Tsar, so that upon returning home, people from every corner of Russia would know the face of their sovereign and protector. But due to disastrously poor planning, something no one had foreseen, the thousands of people gathered on the field with their families and children, upon hearing about the gifts being handed out, surged all at once in a massive stampede toward the single point of distribution. The outcome was horrifying. People were crushed in a barbaric fashion, trampled underfoot, leaving behind, on what was meant to be a day of celebration, the lifeless bodies of thousands of women and children.

The shock caused by this tragedy deeply saddened the Tsar and Tsarina, who wanted to cancel the rest of the day's festivities. But it was not possible. That evening, a grand celebration in honor of the coronation was scheduled to be held at the French Embassy, and the sovereigns' refusal to attend would have been interpreted as an insult to the French people. In the end, for political reasons, the celebration had to go on with the presence of the imperial couple.

The general indignation of the people—outraged upon

hearing that the festivities continued after the previous day's horror—was indescribable. Their beloved "Little Father - The Tsar," had betrayed his people, agreeing to attend a party on that bloodstained day.

"Russia is mourning, and the Tsar is dancing!" was on everyone's mind.

The trust and love of his subjects fell to the lowest depths of respect in their eyes, starting with his first day after coronation. And all signs of misjudgments and bad decisions continued with rumors of assassinations, increasing power the secret police and their camarilla of generals, the loss of the Russo-Japanese War, and the Bloody Sunday of 1905—when thousands more innocent victims were killed in Saint Petersburg—further deepened the people's mistrust and eroded any remaining respect for the Tsar, setting the stage for the revolution of 1917.

Around 1897, before the arrival of the automobile, "Ducky" - Maria's younger sister - and her husband Ernest, the Grand Duke of Hesse, came to visit Romania. King Carol allowed the young royals to receive a few carefully selected friends, approved by the court. Since both princesses were passionate about dancing, they accepted several invitations—of course, with the king's approval— and were accompanied by their husbands, Ernie and Nando.

To entertain her guests, Maria organized a grand masked ball at the Royal Palace, which even the king attended, dressed in a cavalryman's uniform, while the queen came dressed as Dante and recited verses from his work.

In the spring, once the Bucharest ball season had ended, high society would typically gather in the late afternoons along the Şosea – a wide boulevard bordered by chestnut trees and sumptuous villas - riding in carriages pulled by black Russian horses with long, bushy tails. The ladies, dressed in the latest fashions from the style magazines, paraded in their carriages, letting the horses gallop all the way to Lake Băneasa, where construction on the Bucharest racetrack had begun. On the return trip, they allowed the horses to slow down and catch their breath, passing leisurely, greeting acquaintances in other carriages or along the roadside.

In the evenings, Maria and Ducky would go out in their gleaming carriage, driven by a coachman in livery, with a footman seated on the front bench. They gladly received the admiration of passersby, who appreciated the tastefulness of their outfits, their elaborate hats, fashionable sun parasols, and the overall harmony of their color combinations.

Ernie and Nando also rode in a separate carriage, likewise, driven by a liveried coachman and footman, but no entourage could compare with that of the King, who only rarely made public appearances on such outings.

"Those were the best days, I think – the golden era of my life," thought Maria, reminiscent of images and tests of her younger days.

In the mornings, Ducky and Maria often chose the company of officers from the 4th Roșiori Cavalry Regiment under Nando's command. Both women rode thoroughbred horses, galloping wildly along the forest paths on the outskirts of the city, with rest stops that often turned into impromptu parties in a meadow, complete with folk musicians—a surprise arranged by some of the officers. Ernie participated enthusiastically in these youthful escapades, but Nando, shaped by his strict upbringing, was more reluctant to indulge in such pleasures.

At that time, Bucharest was a lively city, and with the opening of Parliament in mid-November, the ball season would begin. Maria and Ducky were always in attendance, either as guests or as hostesses. Dancing was one of their greatest pleasures, and many times they would beg the hosts to allow just one more dance— or a cotillion—after a night full of music, dancing, and flirtation.

Unlike Western European countries, where the Church punished divorcees with excommunication and society viewed any contact with divorced individuals as immoral, Romania and the Orthodox Church held a more lenient attitude, allowing for up to three divorces. Even Queen Elisabeth, acknowledging this social reality, accepted divorced individuals into her circle, though never more than once divorced. Unofficially, however, it was entirely possible for a woman to find herself at a soirée in the company of her former, current, or future lover—each escorted by a different lady.

Around 1908, the Băneasa Hippodrome, located at the far end of Șoseaua Kiseleff, was inaugurated in the presence of the royal family. It quickly became another stage where the Bucharest elite could see and be seen in high society. Each week, at the horse races, ladies and gentlemen of the upper class would gather beneath the covered stands or on the surrounding lawns, binoculars hanging from their necks to follow the races from afar, placing bets or commenting on the value of the competing horses and speculating on the winners.

Not long after the opening of the hippodrome, in 1909, the French aviator Louis Blériot paid a visit and, on October 18th, held a flight demonstration with the airplane he had built. The event caused a great stir not only in Bucharest but throughout the entire country. Until then, no one had seen a motor-powered flying machine—heavier than air. Trains packed with spectators arrived in the capital from all provinces to witness this extraordinary and almost unbelievable spectacle. For a long time afterward, those three flights remained the topic of conversation for every person in the city.

A Decisive Moment

Troubled by pressing matters, King Carol I paced back and forth, hands clasped behind his back, across his study in Peleş Castle, trying to find a solution to the current situation in the Balkans. Romania seemed like an island surrounded by flames on all sides. Peace was out of the question, it had taken all his effort just to maintain neutrality thus far, and even that seemed on the verge of collapsing at any moment. Unable to predict what would happen in the next minute, something had to be done. But what?

In those days, when good news was impossible to come by, it seemed as if the Devil himself had no other task than to stir up the spirits of Romania's neighbors. In 1912, Bulgaria, Serbia, Montenegro, and Greece—united in the Balkan League—declared war on the Ottomans. After their total defeat in the Russo-Turkish War of 1877–1878, in which Romania secured its independence, the Turks never recovered as a major power in Europe. Further proof came in the Italo-Turkish War of 1911–1912, when the Ottomans lost their Tripolitanian, Cyrenaican, and Dodecanese territories, paving the way for the creation of the new state of Libya.

Sensing the moment was ripe, the countries of the southern Balkan Peninsula revolted against the Turks, who still controlled 83% of Europe's territory and 69% of its population, according to statistical internet data. Thus began the First Balkan War in October 1912. The outcome was disastrous for Turkey, which was nearly driven out of Europe after nearly half a millennium of dominance. But this gave rise to a new problem. None of the warring nations had stable borders recognized by their neighbors, having lived under Ottoman occupation for centuries. As a result, their frontiers were fluid, sparking disagreements and conflict among them.

The ink had barely dried on the Treaty of London, signed on May 30, 1913, when the Bulgarians—dissatisfied with how Macedonia had been divided, which they had long coveted—offered the weak justification that their languages were similar. Another motive was their desire for access to the Aegean Sea through the vest side of Salonica's port. On June 29, 1913, King Ferdinand I of Bulgaria ordered a surprise attack on Greece and Serbia. This marked the beginning of the Second Balkan War.

Weary from their campaign against the Ottomans but enraged by their former ally's betrayal, Serbia and Greece responded with force—especially in Greece, where the Bulgarians, outnumbered, were compelled to retreat. Their plan to destroy the Serbian army in Macedonia also failed.

The reason for King Carol's unease had been known for quite some time, going back to the years following Romania's independence, when several states in the region became autonomous principalities. In 1885, when an autonomous principality in the southern Balkans with access to the Aegean Sea—Thrace—was annexed by Bulgaria, nearly doubling its territory, Serbia attacked Bulgaria but was severely defeated. Romania, maintaining neutrality, stepped in as a mediator in the conflict, and peace was established in 1886 in Bucharest, placing, for the first time, the name of the new kingdom's capital, Bucharest, on the map of Europe's major cities.

At the same time, the formation of a large and powerful Bulgaria in the Balkans concerned the Romanian king. On one hand, there was the fear that the Bulgarians might attempt to reclaim Dobruja, which had been added to Romania in 1878 in exchange for the three southern Bessarabia counties—Ismail, Cahul, and Bolgrad—taken by the Russians. On the other hand, to maintain the balance of power in the region, Bulgaria would need to give up certain heavily Romanian-populated territories south of Silistra.

King Carol stopped pacing the room and came to a halt in front of his desk:

"This cannot stand! The Serbs have always been on our side. They will be with us when the time comes to bring Transylvania back into the arms of the nation. We cannot sit idly by! King Ferdinand of Bulgaria has gone too far by attacking his neighbors! And now he thinks he can stretch across the entire Balkan region?

Why? By what right? This is too much!", declared the king.

"What is to be done?", asked Prince Ferdinand, who had calmly observed the tension spreading around his uncle's face.

Everyone listened intently. No one knew the best course of action, except for Take Ionescu[xvi], the Minister of Internal Affairs and the most hawkish among them. He had long maintained that *"we must march through Bulgaria to reach Transylvania!"* His public pressure—in Parliament, in the press, and through rallies—was well known. King Carol's desire to maintain a neutral stance was vehemently combated by him.

Prince Ferdinand continued to observe King Carol's face—aged, bend a little, dressed in military attire, but with a determined bearing. In front of him stood Prime Minister Titu Maiorescu[xvii], leader of the *Junimea* group of aspiring young writers, Take Ionescu, Alexandru Marghiloman, the Minister of Finance, and others.

"We must march into Bulgaria!", declared the king. "I see no other solution. I didn't want us to get involved in this war. You know better than anyone that from the beginning of the First War, you wanted us to fight alongside them against the Turks. I was the one who opposed it!", the king said, looking directly at Take Ionescu.

"Yes, Your Majesty! If I may—indeed, that is so! I currently have an open channel with one of the Bulgarian parliamentarians, Stoian Danev, with whom I have discussed the fact that it is in their interest to cede to Romania the region in southern Dobruja, inhabited by Romanians and others who speak our language. He, too, saw that after we connected Dobruja to Romanian territory via the Saligny Bridge at Cernavoda, their chances of reclaiming the area vanished. Therefore…"

"There's no time for that now! We declare war on Bulgaria and march in!"

Titu Maiorescu rose from his chair, clearing his throat:

"With Your Majesty's permission, by July 3rd I will present the Royal Decree for the Mobilization of the Romanian Army for approval!"

On that day—July 3, 1913—the king was in Corabia to witness the Romanian army's parade as it crossed pontoon bridges set up across the Danube between Măgura and Bechet. With the sovereign were Prince Ferdinand and his wife, Princess Maria. On the same date came news that, at Kilkis, the Bulgarian troops—who had held the plains below—suffered massive losses in the face of the Greek offensive. Full mobilization was enacted on July 5, 1913, and on that same day, King Carol appointed Prince Ferdinand as Commander of the Operational Army in the Balkan War.

On July 7, Romania officially delivered its Declaration of

War to Bulgaria, proclaiming that it had no intention of subjugating the country's political structure or defeating the Bulgarian army. The Romanian government expressed its solidarity with the international concern for limiting bloodshed. On the day of the declaration, 80,000 troops from the 5th Army Corps entered Dobruja, securing the Turtucaia–Balchik front.

Upon hearing the news, the public reacted with elation. Nearly all the newspapers of the time reflected the people's enthusiastic approval. In Bucharest, as crowds showered flowers on the troops marching toward the border, reports came in that the Bulgarians were retreating in the face of Greek and Serbian advances.

Precautionary Measures

In 1901, when 38-year-old Ion Cantacuzino returned to the country after his studies at the Pasteur Institute in Paris—where he became an assistant to the renowned Professor Ilya Mechnikov in the field of immune system mechanisms—his name was already broadly known. He had previously earned in Paris the title of Doctor of Medicine after presenting his thesis entitled *Research on the Mechanism of Destruction of the Cholera Vibrio in the Body*. But his studies were not limited to medicine only; they also had strong ties to biology, and not least, to entomology, the study of insects and their relationship with nature, humans, and other organisms. This breadth of expertise, combined with several articles and studies in the area of specialty, led to his appointment as Professor of Experimental Medicine at the Faculty of Medicine in Bucharest and, later, as Director General of the Romanian Public Health Service.

Now in 1912, reviewing all the news, articles in the press, and medical journals about the spread of cholera among Serbian, Bulgarian, and Turkish soldiers during the Balkan War against the Ottoman Empire—a conflict in which Romania was not part—he felt he could not simply stand by. If the disease were to cross the border and reach across the Danube, the population of our country would need to be prepared with effective countermeasures. For this reason, he called Dr. Constantin Ionescu-Mihăiești in to address the issue.

"You know, I believe the news," started Dr Cantacuzino, showing his colleague a seat in his office. "I've come to think that regarding the situation in Bulgaria, which is far from encouraging, we need a closer look to see what is happening there. Cholera cases among the soldiers on both sides of the front are increasing, and the hygiene and isolation measures for the sick are inadequate. As far as we're concerned, I'd like to send a team of specialists and students from medicine, biology, and epidemiology to study the epidemic in Bulgaria and collect strains of cholera vibrio to prepare a cholera vaccine here as a preventive measure. What do you think?"

"Professor, I totally agree with you. I believe the mission you speak of should be undertaken immediately, and if you don't object, I would like to take part personally in assembling the team. We need to prepare a cholera vaccine that both civilian and military health services can be equipped with."

Following this conversation, a team composed of specialists and students travelled to Bulgaria under the leadership of Dr. Constantin Ionescu-Mihăiești with the mission of studying cholera cases and collecting vibrio strains to enable the mass production of a cholera vaccine in Romania. This effort laid the foundation for developing large-scale culture methods that would be used in the event of an epidemic in the country.

In January 1913, at the request of Professor Ion Cantacuzino, the Ministry of War—through Decision No. 39—introduced the chemical water analysis kit and the mobile bacteriological laboratory as standard equipment for the army's medical units.

The cholera vaccine and timely preventive measures taken shortly after the epidemic's outbreak successfully halted its spread within the Romanian army before the troops returned home in the Second Balkan War. Romania became the first country in the world to successfully combat cholera through a scientific and organized response.

The Conscription

A vast courtyard, flanked by old buildings whose crimson walls were beginning to peel. At the large gate opening onto the road, a sentry stood with his rifle slung over his shoulder, watching the people coming and going with disinterest, and only at the passing of an officer, he would snap to a stand-up position.

At a table outside one of the buildings, a few soldiers sat with papers in front of them, jotting down information from the men filing past:

"Name, soldier?"

"Tudor Avădanei!"

"Place of birth?"

"Copăceni, Ilfov!"

"Date of birth?"

"March 19th, 1879!"

"Your father's name?"

"Ion Constantinescu!"

"Then why are you Avădanei and he's Constantinescu?"

"He died on the front at Vidin in 1878, the year I was born!"

"I see. What's your mother's name?"

"Ecaterina Constantinescu was a teacher."

"Is she still alive?"

"No."

"Married?"

"Widower."

"Children?"

"None."

"Any training?"

"What do you mean?"

"Did you do military service?"

"Yes, like everyone else. In my youth..."

"Where?"

"In the infantry."

"What rank were you discharged with?"

"Corporal."

"Alright. Go to the medical exam line—the one on the right!"

Tudor joined the line. There were about thirty men ahead of

him. He'd left his village early that morning, a knapsack slung over his shoulder with a few changes of clothes in case he needed them, and some food. He'd arranged the night before with old man Vasile, who had business in town, to ride with him in his cart. They reached the market town just before noon. Tudor thanked the man for the lift and began asking around for the garrison he was supposed to report to. It was already late, and the crowd outside was still large.

Tired and dusty, some men smoked, others dozed on small crates they had brought from home to carry food and clothing. One man with a curled black mustache, leaning against a wall, pulled a pocketknife from his coat and began sharpening the blade on a stone he found on the ground.

"What are you doing with that pebble? It's not exactly a whetstone."

"It'll do until I find a better one!"

The line moved forward a step closer to the door, but time took long until a few more people were called in.

"Hey, comrade, got a match?" asked a young man in front of Tudor.

"I don't smoke!"

"Damn it! I had some, but the corporal at the back table asked for my matchbox and never gave it back".

"Not a big loss… Look, that guy behind me is smoking. You can light yours from his."

"Thanks!"

The young man lit his cigarette and returned to his place in line. He was dressed, like Tudor, in town clothes, but his were finer—shiny, polished shoes and necktie. He looked like a merchant, a clerk, or maybe a university student. Around them were people of all kinds—some older, some younger, villagers in traditional clothing, even with *opinci* (leather peasant soles tied around feet with straps) on their feet, while others clearly came from the city. It was hot, stifling, and the wait dragged on.

"Where are you from?" the young man asked Tudor.

"From Copăceni, not far from Bucharest! You?"

"I'm from the city! I live with my parents."

"Not married?

"No. I'm just engaged. Her parents think it's better to wait until the war is over."

"Afraid you'll find someone else in the meantime?"

"I think they're afraid I won't come back…"

"I'm Tudor. What's your name?"

"Izu Haimovici".

"You're Jewish?"

"Yes".

"And you think they'll accept you?"

"Why wouldn't they? Am I not a citizen too?"

"Sure, but nearsighted people are citizens as well, and they're still not accepted…"

"But I'm not nearsighted. What do they have to do with me?"

"I don't know. You're different—you're a *jidan* (pejorative name given to Jews in Romania). Sorry for putting it like that".

"You're wrong! I'm a *jidan* because I have a different religion, but I'm Romanian because I was born here just like you, and no one can prove they love this country more than I do. And if you must know, my fiancée's parents won't let me marry their daughter for the same reason—because I'm Jewish and she's Christian. That's not fair!"

"Don't be upset", Tudor tried to calm the young man. "I didn't make those rules…"

"I know you didn't, but tell me this—why is it that I, as a Jew, can't be a patriot, yet a German king can be? What makes him more Romanian than I am, born right here? Huh? You want to know why I became a Romanian citizen, when not all Jews have that right? Because my father fought in the war against the Turks in '77! That's why!"

"Yeah, well, my father gave his life there! He died for independence!" Tudor replied.

"And mine fought for independence, too! Many died. Many survived. That was their fate! Independence demanded sacrifices..."

Tudor said nothing more. A few men behind him started muttering:

"Did you hear that one? See how the Jews slither in? Now they want to steal our independence too!"

Tudor overheard them and shot them a look that silenced them. The man leaning against the wall, still holding his pocketknife, found a piece of wood and began carving off thin shavings with the sharpened blade.

"Listen here, Itzik! You know why they won't take you in? Because we don't trust your lot. You'd sell us out for thirty pieces of silver! That's why it's better you stay home..."

Izu looked like he was about to respond to the man with the pocketknife but stopped when Tudor spoke up.

"I think we'd better just mind our own business! Let the higher-ups decide what's best! It's not up to us".

At that moment, another group was called into the examination room, and the line moved forward a few more steps. After the medical check and shower, they were issued their military gear. Some tunics were clean, but not new—they looked like reissued stock. The boots were the worst part, a mix of old and new, and it was hard to tell what size they were supposed to be. Carrying their gear in their arms, they were marched to a hall outfitted with bunk beds lined along the walls from one end to the other. Tudor chose a top bunk and placed his things on it.

Once they were dressed in uniform, Tudor looked around at everyone and couldn't shake the thought that now they all looked the same. Before, you could tell by someone's clothes if they were a peasant, a laborer, or an educated man—like Izu seemed to be. But now, shaved and dressed in army uniform, they were indistinguishable from one another, a compact mass of people with no difference between them, except for the ranks on their shoulders. They had been made uniform.

They were ordered to line up in the corridor, along the edge of their beds. Tudor also noticed that the bunk next to his had been taken by Izu. The man with the pocketknife had settled into the bed below Izu's and shouted out loud enough for everyone nearby to hear:

"Hey Itzik! You don't still wet the bed at night, do you?" Everyone burst into loud laughter.

"I don't know, no guarantees!" said Izu. "Better keep an umbrella handy, just in case!"

This time, no one laughed. Lined up in pairs in front of the door, a boy was appointed to stand guard in the room, while the rest were taken to the mess hall for dinner.

"This is where the unraveling starts," thought Tudor bringing his plate to a long table with benches along sides, next to Izu.

At the Head of the Soldiers

That morning, Maria had risen early. She was restless, barely able to keep calm enough to enjoy her breakfast in the garden of Cotroceni Palace, the princely residence built by the King for the young couple. She was already dressed for the parade, ready to take her place at the head of her 4th Roșiori Cavalry Regiment, over which King Carol I had appointed her Honorary Commander. Nando had once commanded this regiment, but now not only this unit—the entire army—was under his command. He had left, along with the entire general staff, to prepare the crossing of the troops over the Danube.

The honor of being named Honorary Commander had lit up the young princess's life years ago, on a charming day of Autumn in 1897, four years after her marriage to Ferdinand. It had indeed been a great joy and distinction, especially because Nando had also been promoted to the rank of colonel when he was given command of that regiment, located near their new residence at Cotroceni. Before that promotion, he had served in the Mountain Hunters Regiment at Sinaia, wearing the same dark ochre uniform he had worn on the day of their wedding in Sigmaringen.

Knowing how much Maria loved animals, horseback riding, and the outdoors, Nando had one day asked Maria:

"Why don't you come to the barracks and take part in the marches alongside us?"

"I would like to, but you think that Uncle and the Court would approve such action?"

"We'll see. So, you come?"

"With great pleasure!"

The effect of her appearance on the soldiers in the regiment was indescribable: the cavalcades among the officers, their delight, and the cheers of the troops in the garrison were full of enthusiasm.

The event marking the conferral of that honorary title had taken place at Sinaia, at the royal summer residence of Peleș Castle. The princess used to go for morning rides there, mounted on a magnificent Circassian horse, a gift from her cousin on her mother's side, Prince Boris Vladimirovich. He was visiting Romania at the same time as Maria's brother, Alfred. Both had come as guests and had been present at the ceremony. No one had expected such a surprise, especially Maria, more used to a rebuke from the king, rather than such an elevation.

Usually, the mornings in Sinaia were refreshed by the mist through which the sun added more color to the meadows and fir trees all around. The air felt fresh and invigorating. Maria was returning from a wild ride through the woods that crown the town. King Carol often took walks along the paths behind the castle, and his route would frequently intersect with Maria's, who came galloping down from the mountain slopes, accompanied by her pedigree dogs running behind her.

"Beautiful day, splendid weather!" the king would say instead of a greeting[xviii].

"Yes, uncle, and the forest is so beautiful! No forest is as majestic as Sinaia's."

"Where have you been?"

"Oh, there are paths everywhere!"

"Yes, yes, but be careful—your horse jumps a bit wildly!"

"Yes, but it climbs like a deer," Maria would reply, waving to him as she galloped off toward the castle.

Her uncle wasn't inclined to encourage the young princess's exuberance, but at the same time, Maria could see in his eyes that he admired her youthful spirit and her courage to venture alone into the solitude of the woods and surrounding mountains. More than once, the king had to endure—something quite unusual for him—the boldness with which she challenged some of his decisions, not entirely illogically, though he would often dismiss her arguments simply because she didn't know the reasons he couldn't ignore.

Lately, however, seeing that his nephew Ferdinand was

always willing to accept any decision as if it were a command—even though the king knew he wasn't a fool—Carol had begun to doubt his ability to choose and decide what ought to be done. In Ferdinand's docility, the king did not see the same sense of direction and initiative that he couldn't help but notice in Maria. For this reason, he began to pay more attention to his niece, trying to explain to her some of the concerns that troubled him.

In recent months, Maria had suffered a terrible case of phlebitis, which confined her to bed for nearly three months, following the birth of her sixth child, Mircea, in January. Her uncle came to visit:

"How were you doing? Still, it hearts you?"

"I hope it will pass soon."

"Good, good. You must take care of yourself!"

He himself, now aged and ailing, would come after finishing his duties—usually in the evening—sit beside her bed, and start sharing the difficulties he faced. Often, for political or other reasons, his wishes and plans had to be postponed or even abandoned entirely—not because he wanted to, but to appease opinions different than his own. He looked tired and disappointed.

As if these confidences were being shared with a peer of equal rank—or with his own self—the old king, without regard for the difference between them, the uncle and the princess seemed during these talks like a grandfather passing stories to his granddaughter. Even more curious was the fact that these conversations no longer bored Maria as they once had, back when she had just arrived in Romania, and he and Ferdinand would sit in their palace apartment discussing political matters she neither understood nor cared to understand.

The Cotroceni Palace, rebuilt by the king for the princely family, stood at the edge of the city, near an immense park filled with ancient trees—a true forest transformed, just a few years before they moved to Cotroceni, into a beautiful botanical garden. Nando was absolutely delighted by this garden and the quiet surrounding, especially because he was a great lover of plants, flowers, and nature. On training days, his cavalry regiment would ride along the road separating Cotroceni Palace from the park, heading toward the nearby training plateau—an area that would later come to be known as Militari.

The uniform of the 4th Roşiori Cavalry Regiment consisted of red tunics with black trim, gilded buttons, and black trousers on regular days—white ones on special occasions. Maria had a similar riding outfit made for herself, which she wore with pride at the head of the regiment each time. Her only difference between outfits was that instead of trousers, she wore long riding skirts suited for riding side-saddle. When the king saw her, he would often tease:

"So, are we wearing white trousers or black ones today?[xix]"

But this day, the road would be different. At the head of her 4th Roșiori Cavalry Regiment, Maria would ride all the way to the city limits. Behind them, the lines would be followed by cannons drawn by horses, auxiliary services, wagons laden with supplies, ammunition, equipment, and even some field ambulances. Following pre-established routes, the columns moved down roadways lined with onlookers, their gazes full of admiration, their arms tossing flowers, their voices cheering with joy, and their hearts lifted by the blessings offered by reverent priests from the roadside. Young girls from nearby schools bashfully lowered their eyes whenever a mounted officer urged them to hop up into the saddle with him. Among all these people by the roadside, some mothers with tears gleaming in their eyes would murmur a prayer for the young soldiers to return safely home.

At a Crossroad

At seventy-four, King Carol could feel that the vigor and energy of his youth—when anything he set his mind to was not only possible but guaranteed—had begun to abandon him. His determined nature, which had never allowed itself to be overwhelmed by doubts or hardships, had once ensured the success of any plan. Nothing was impossible for him. But now, things are different. He stood alone by the window in his office at Peleş Castle thinking:

"Oh, dear God! I feel so old now. Worries, ill health, and my age are turned against me today. Even if I dare to lead my troops on this campaign in Bulgaria - God, You only Knoweth - how much I would like to do it, but I'm no longer as I was years back, in 1877, when my energy and drive of those days faded away."

Back then, in that battle, he didn't only command the Romanian forces, but also those of Russia with their line of generals and advisers listening to his orders. From the height of a cannon carriage, surrounded by the roar of nearby shellfire, he commanded the entire course of the battles that brought him victory at Plevna, followed by those at Smârdan and Vidin, that had opened the path to the country's liberation from Ottoman rule. The Turks were forced to acknowledge the triumph of the Romanians by signing the Treaty of San Stefano. That treaty, and later the Treaty of Berlin in 1878, recognized the independence of Romania, Serbia, and Montenegro, and granted autonomy to Bulgaria.

Now, however, it seemed no one remembered those accomplishments, and the king's confidence in Romania's victory hung in the balance—because it no longer depended on him.

"What is to be done?" asked the king. "A decision must be made in a hurry, and there is no choice but to let someone - a younger man with less experience - like my nephew Ferdinand and the generals lead the army."

The thought that he could not be there with them to see everything, to direct, to coordinate, and give orders dictated by the circumstances of war, was a painful, inconsolable burden for His Majesty. Leaving the windows, Carol moved slowly around the room and finally sat at his desk.

"What else could I do?" he asked himself, with a sad smile. "That is life, and I must surrender to its will!"

Once, in his youth, Carol had been a constant optimist, confident in the power of order and discipline. In his family, these two virtues had shaped generations of soldiers, guided by a spirit of honor and justice. The best example was his own father, Prince Karl Anton of Hohenzollern-Sigmaringen. At that time, Germany was divided between many strongholds competing for a leadership role.

In the midst of the 1848 Revolution, together with Prince Friedrich Wilhelm of Hohenzollern-Hechingen, the two eldest branches of the Hohenzollern family had renounced their sovereign rights on December 7, 1849, in the hope of bringing about a unified Germany.

Among Prince Karl Anton's four children, Carol—second in line after Leopold, who is now Nando's father—was the only one to inherit the firm character and iron will of their father along with his political skill.

In Romania, after Prince Alexandru Ioan Cuza was dethroned from power following a conspiracy on February 11, 1866, when neglect and corruption could not be tolerated anymore, a public plebiscite was held to bring in a foreign ruler, one who would not be entangled in local intrigues. At the time, nearly all European states were ruled by foreign monarchs. Prime Minister I.C. Brătianu had traveled to Sigmaringen specifically to persuade Prince Carol of Hohenzollern to accept the offer of the Romanian throne on Good Friday, 1866[xx]. Carol knew that the little eastern country was challenged by many problems and assumed a large responsibility, taking on this offer. But encouraged by family, and even Emperor Napoleon III —related to Carol—who advocated for him in France's name, he hastened to take on the leadership of the Romanian country.

Because of the ongoing war between Germany and Austria,

Prince Carol had to travel incognito, using a Swiss passport under an assumed name and avoiding Austrian territory. He arrived in Bucharest on May 10, 1866, on a rainy day.

At Băneasa railway station, he was greeted with bread and salt, according to Romanian tradition. He was presented with the key to the city, and everyone considered his arrival on such a rainy day to be a providential sign of good fortune. On that occasion, Carol took his oath of loyalty before the country's officials:

"I swear to uphold the laws of Romania, to defend her rights and territorial integrity!"

When he accepted the throne, Carol understood Romania was not on par with the countries of Western Europe. But what he found there surpassed even the darkest picture he had imagined. The country lagged behind the West by at least a century. The treasury was empty, civil servants' salaries went unpaid, the army was disorganized, lacked ammunition, and was completely devoid of discipline. Poverty was visible everywhere, food was scarce, and not a single railroad line existed.

In the countryside, things were no better. The agrarian reform introduced by the former ruler, Cuza, had left both peasants and landowners dissatisfied. When landowners personally managed their estates, peasants, though burdened by hard labor, maintained a human, even understanding relationship with their lords. But once the big cities' lifestyle, and elegance of life abroad, became a fashionable sign of richness, landowners abandoned their estates to be run by intermediaries—leaseholders whose job was to generate enough profit to cover not only the landlords' increasingly extravagant expenses but also their own.

The lives of the peasants deteriorated rapidly. Their obligations increased, and so did the taxes. Carol understood all of this.

"It was clear to me that something had to be done to improve their situation. I also knew how farms were managed in Germany, but there was no time to spend on this problem. More urgent issues came first."

At the beginning, due to an unclear text in the accord, the guaranteeing powers had reluctantly accepted the election of the same ruler in both Wallachia and Moldavia in the person of Colonel Alexandru Ioan Cuza. However, when Prince Carol arrived in Romania, those same powers were not so favorable to the idea of uniting the two principalities under a single ruler. The strongest opposition came from Austria-Hungary, newly formed in 1865, which also controlled Transylvania—a region with a large Romanian population that was harshly oppressed by the Hungarians.

The Turks, on the other hand, immediately expressed their disapproval, massing troops on the southern bank of the Danube. To calm the Pasha, Carol urgently traveled to Constantinople to discuss Romania's vassal status. Ali Pasha received the Romanian Prince at court with great honors and festivities. Pasha presented him with a sword and a belt adorned with gold and diamonds. Carol quickly realized that these gifts were not given out of respect for his new role as ruler of Romania, but because he belonged to the Hohenzollern family[xxi]. Through careful diplomacy, he not only secured the goodwill of the Ottoman Porte but also won the right to mint his own military decorations, bearing his likeness.

Back in the country, within just 55 days of his arrival, this 27-year-old man, Carol, drafted Romania's first constitution, in 1866[xxii], a document with democratic provisions enshrined in law. On June 29, Parliament passed the new constitution, which guaranteed freedom of conscience, of the press, of education, the right to public assembly, equality before the law, and voting rights for those who paid taxes to the government.

The new constitution also established the hereditary right of Carol's male descendants—raised in the Orthodox faith—to succeed him. Also, he was named Supreme Commander of the Romanian Army, with the right to conduct negotiations with other states. Legislative power was shared between the ruler and the two parliamentary branches, the Chamber of Deputies and the Senate, but citizenship rights were granted only to those belonging to the

Christian faith.

The early years of his reign were not without challenges. A year after his marriage, in 1869, to Princess Elisabeth of Wied, Romania's financial situation became critical—even dire—due to the Franco-Prussian War of 1870–1871, which prevented the export of grain and other goods, despite a bountiful harvest that year. Every bad news affecting the country, even the ones happening outside his power to change their course, was blamed on him.

Dissatisfaction mounted, and scandals erupted over the misallocation of railway funds. Frequent government changes occurred within short periods in expectation of calming the tensions. Most notably, the Romanian people's sympathy for the French cause in the war—contrary to that of the prince, in whose veins ran German blood—culminated in a short-lived revolt of one day. Leading liberal politicians such as I.C. Brătianu, C.A. Rosetti, and others were involved. Known as the "Republic of Ploieşti,[xxiii]" this attempt to strip the prince of power, copying the same scenario as in the case of dethroning Cuza, was quashed in less than 24 hours by the conservative prime minister Manole Costache Iepureanu and ended with the arrest of those involved. When later he was informed that none of the participants was punished, Carol was saddened because the judges followed the same rule applied after the conspiration against Cuza.

Nevertheless, nothing deterred the ruler from continuing his plans for organizing and modernizing the country. With a strong sense of self-confidence, paired with the foresight of a prudent and wise politician—firm but not malicious or biased—Carol believed in his right to rule justly and without abuse. He was aware of one thing and believed it deeply: that of all the truths presented to him, only his own mattered most—because it was weighed and considered in a scrupulous judgement of all the factors known only to him.

After Romania gained independence from the Ottomans in 1878, the European powers became suspicious of the new rights assumed by Russia through the Peace Treaty of San Stefano and refused to recognize it. Bismarck—the towering statesman of the era, who held the cards of Europe's destiny in his hands like in a never-ending poker game with the world's great powers—called the Congress of Berlin, held in June and July 1878. Germany, England, France, Austria-Hungary, Russia, and Turkey all took part.

Representing Romania, Prime Minister I.C. Brătianu and Foreign Minister Mihail Kogălniceanu addressed the Congress on June 1, 1878. They requested the recognition of Romania's independence, the preservation of its national integrity, which included the southern territories of Bessarabia, granted to Romania by the Treaty of Paris in 1856, but claimed by Russia now. Romania's neutrality was also declared at the Congress.

In response, the Congress[xxiv] made its recognition of Romania's independence conditional on the resolution of one issue: the granting of citizenship rights to the country's non-Christian population, particularly the Jews. At the time, they were deprived of many essential civil rights: They were not allowed to vote, they could not own property, could not sign contracts, and were forbidden to engage in the trade of food.

Weighing this request, Kogălniceanu and Prime Minister Brătianu objected to the lack of integration of the Jews from Bessarabia into the culture and customs of the rest of the country. They proposed that citizenship be granted to Jews on a case-by-case basis, individually, not to all at once in a collective act. In line with this approach, the Chamber of Deputies decreed the granting of citizenship to a group of 900 Jewish families who had taken an active part in the War of Independence. For the rest, citizenship would be granted upon request, subject to parliamentary approval.

The situation remained unsettled. The Congress awarded Russia the fertile southern lands of Bessarabia contrary to the Romanian request. As a result, the Congress redrew Romania's borders, offering as compensation the arid territory of Dobruja, south of the Danube Delta, with access to the Black Sea. As there was still no guarantee regarding recognition of Romanian independence, the ambassador to Vienna, Ion Bălăceanu, a former Foreign Minister and a diplomat with strong ties to France and

England, negotiated separately the official recognition of Romania's independence with Austria-Hungary, which was eager to establish commercial relations with Romania. In this way, the other powers were compelled to recognize Romania's independence and national sovereignty.

When the Romanian troops returned home after the war, on October 8, 1878, they marched in parade beneath the Arch of Triumph[xxv], erected in their honor as a temporary wooden structure—a tribute to the victories achieved on the battlefield.

On March 15, 1881, the Constitution was amended to proclaim the Kingdom of Romania. Prince Carol became the first king—King Carol I—and his heirs were to bear the title of royal princes. The king's coronation took place on May 10, 1881, on the 15th Anniversary Day of his arrival in his new country. The royal crown, forged from the barrel of a captured Ottoman cannon and turned into a symbol of monarchy, was never worn by the king. He justified his refusal to wear it by stating:

"I became King, and the Principalities of Romania became a Kingdom, thanks to the battles and sacrifices endured by the Romanian people—not by Divine grace."

During the 47 years following his arrival in the country, up to the summer of 1913, King Carol's reign brought Romania numerous brilliant achievements in nearly every field of activity.

These accomplishments might have been even greater had the advisors on whom he relied on been more persistent in pursuing some of the reforms the country needed - reforms he did not always grasp, having been raised with a different mentality. It's not hard to see, looking back, how many problems wouldn't have come to light if someone were able to let him know beforehand what the country thinks. But by lack of interest, fear, or stupidity, no one made him aware of some difficult situations. As an absolute monarch, whenever he sensed growing public unrest, Carol would replace the sitting government with the opposition party, blaming the former for the discontent.

The National Liberal Party represented the middle class, the bourgeoisie, small merchants, and a significant number of boyars and small industrialists—who sought to modernize the country through industrialization and trade. After the death of Ion C. Brătianu in 1891—a veteran of the 1848 revolution—other leaders followed at the helm of the party: C.A. Rosetti and Dimitrie Sturdza, a former secretary to Alexandru Ioan Cuza. He later became President of the Romanian Academy.

Opposing the Liberals, the Conservative Party was backed by the large landowners—the boyars—who supported agrarian issues from the perspective of landowners rather than of the masses of peasants who worked their lands. Leading this party was Lascar Catargiu, who was called upon to restore order whenever the

Liberals' pursuit of modernization grew too excessive. Among the noteworthy Conservatives were Gheorghe Cantacuzino—nicknamed "The Nabob", Petre Carp, Alexandru Marghiloman, and Titu Maiorescu, who founded the literary and cultural society "Junimea."

In 1913, after 47 years of King Carol I's reign over a country that, at the time of his arrival, had stood at the fringes of Europe—largely unknown and internally plagued by the vices of corruption, bribery, and the relentless pursuit of power or quick enrichment—Romania had undergone a remarkable transformation. With the creation of a modern industrial base and the development of transport infrastructure, including roads, railways, the telegraph, and electricity—the entire country experienced significant progress.

In the cultural sphere, starting from the second half of the 19th century, Romania flourished with first-rate writers such as Negruzzi, Alecsandri, and Grigore Alexandrescu. The dawn of the 20th century brought an explosion of literary talent, who crystallized and enriched the Romanian language, creating works of high stylistic achievement in both prose and poetry. Mihail Eminescu, Coșbuc, Vlahuță, Creangă, Odobescu, and Caragiale produced singular works that reflected the national spirit of the Romanian people, on par with the creations of the great European and global literary geniuses.

Likewise, internationally acclaimed painters such as Grigorescu and Andreescu emerged, alongside sculptors of Brancusi's stature and musicians like Enescu, who sowed the seeds for future generations of remarkable Romanian artists in the interwar period.

Urban development was another area of growth: in nearly all the country's major cities, new roads and boulevards were laid, alongside impressive cultural and historical monuments, parks, and statues of distinguished personalities. In 1906, on the occasion of King Carol I's 40th anniversary on the throne, the Bucharest International Exhibition was inaugurated—a brilliant showcase of the country's accomplishments and a celebration of the exceptional results achieved nationwide in those years.

Among the economic achievements, the new petroleum industry was born, more than three thousand kilometers of railway were built, and navigation on the Danube was expanded—particularly at the Iron Gates, where numerous rocks were removed. The Saligny Bridge at Cernavodă was constructed, linking Dobruja to the rest of the country. Universities, hospitals, new schools, and public buildings—such as the National Theatre and the Romanian Athenaeum—were erected in the capital, in Iaşi, and across the country, their architecture and beauty rivaling the finest creations of the West.

"Yes, there were undoubtedly many achievements during these 47 years of rule," thought King Carol, after briefly reviewing the accomplishments amassed over that time.

" But there were also matters completely neglected. Among them, the poverty of the poorer class, the peasants. Failures to address them sparked public discontent, death, and heartbreaking sorrow."

Always preoccupied with other problems, never granted a moment's respite in a world constantly in motion and full of unrest, disputes, and wars, King Carol had failed to notice that most of his people, the peasantry, were sinking deeper into poverty and hunger, with no one to defend them. The rural population was growing rapidly, but at the same time, infant mortality had reached some of the highest rates in Europe. The land reform[xxvi] carried out during Cuza's reign had granted only small, insufficient plots of land, leaving many peasants to work the boyars' estates in exchange for wages paid in kind.

While eight out of ten inhabitants lived in villages, six out of ten peasants owned very little land—or none at all. Of the 6.3 million hectares of arable land used for agriculture, three million were owned by just 6,500 boyars, the remainder divided among the rest of the peasants. Romania had become a major exporter of agricultural goods in Europe, but the increase in volume did not bring a corresponding rise in income. On the contrary, it deepened the peasants' dissatisfaction, as they were forced to renew land lease contracts from estate managers at ever-increasing prices. Thus began the first uprisings of peasants in northern Moldavia in 1907.

The revolt spread to Oltenia, creating the impression that the entire country was in flames. Fields, homes, manors, and various other buildings belonging to the upper class were set ablaze. The rebellion continued to spread, and when news arrived from Transylvania that Austria-Hungary was massing troops at the border—fearing the uprising might cross into their territory—King Carol called on the Conservative government led by Gheorghe Cantacuzino to act immediately. The government resigned on March 10, 1907. A new Liberal government was formed under Dimitrie Sturdza. Together with the Minister of War, General Averescu, they quelled the uprising with drastic measures, mobilizing 140,000 soldiers and issuing orders to open fire, resulting in the deaths of over 10,000 peasants to restore peace.

The world was shaken by the news of these events; Romania's prestige suffered a heavy blow, and many intellectuals such as Nicolae Iorga, Alexandru Vlahuță, Ion Luca Caragiale, Dobrogeanu-Gherea, and Radu Rosetti, protested the violent repression. The government began to introduce a series of reforms to ease relations between peasants and landowners, setting maximum rental prices for land and minimum wages for agricultural workers. Still, the core problem remained unresolved. Only years later, in 1913, the progressive youth of the Liberal Party, seeking a permanent solution to the peasant crisis, appealed to Ionel Brătianu—the son of the great statesman I.C. Brătianu—to take leadership of the party and implement the reforms necessary to improve the situation in agriculture.

The King held a fondness for the young politician Ionel Brătianu, who was open, direct, and honest, demonstrating good judgment and a clear grasp of political issues. His preference for the young man became evident. During the king's periods of convalescence, brought on by recurring liver crises that confined him to bed and drained him due to the strict diet prescribed by doctors, Carol began confiding in his niece, Princess Marie, about his impressions of Ionel Brătianu—especially in contrast to his predecessor, Dimitrie Sturdza:

"Nowadays, working with Ionel Brătianu is a relief for me," he would say.

A similar affection the king began to feel toward his niece, particularly after the 1907 uprising, when he noticed a genuine shift in her attitude, a deeper maturity and an effort to better understand the core of the country's problems. With her, Ferdinand, and a few young politicians befriending them, the future seems brighter.

On July 3, 1913, astride his horse, the king watched

pensively as his troops paraded through Corabia, just before crossing to the opposite bank of the Danube, into Bulgaria. The soldiers, elated by the presence of their sovereign—accompanied by Prince Ferdinand, Princess Marie, officers, and dignitaries—burst into endless cheers that echoed along the pontoon bridge stretching between the two riverbanks.

This scene, a reenactment of the earlier crossing into Bulgaria back in 1877, was deeply familiar to him. He felt the same fierce resolve for battle, just as he had witnessed in Plevna. He himself longed to cross the river once more at the head of his troops. But now, history had assigned him a minor role, that of a mere spectator to all that was about to unfold across the battlefield, where, contrary to expectations, no shots were fired, no resistance met them on the opposite shore. With tearful eyes, he watched his soldiers cross the Danube, offering them his blessing and heartfelt wishes for success in battle.

In March

"Dear Father,

Kissing your hand, I hope these lines find you and mother priestess in good health and good spirits. We've arrived safely in the land of the Bulgarians, and the people here have received us peacefully and without hostility. So far, we haven't fired a single shot, as we haven't been confronted by any army. We're advancing cautiously toward their capital, Sofia.

When we crossed the Danube into Bulgaria on a military pontoon bridge stretching from one bank to the other, I saw His Majesty King Carol I, accompanied by Prince Ferdinand, Princess Marie, and other dignitaries. The King had come to see his troops, and we rewarded him with cheers of joy. The Princess and her entourage saluted us smartly with their hands to their caps, but the King observed us in solemn silence, full of dignity.

Princess Marie looked just like the lady who laid flowers at Vasilica's grave, but I couldn't be sure—it was hard to tell since she wore a military uniform. I keep wondering if the lady I talked to was really the Princess.

I also cannot stop thinking that my poor father might be buried somewhere around here, but where would I even begin to find his grave? I've noticed that here, the households in the villages we marched through are better off than those at home, but there are also signs of devastation left by last year's war. I see many houses burned or abandoned, livestock left without owners, and people staying hidden indoors.

We're faring rather poorly with food. We march from morning until night, and our supplies have fallen far behind us. It's hard for them to catch up, especially with this mountainous terrain and the tough uphill climbs. The locals tend to avoid us, and there's no way to find anything to eat. I hope the war ends soon and we can return home quickly.

Please give my respects to mother priestess and Aunt Ileana—tell them that I kiss their hands—and send my greetings to those you see from the village.

With love,

Tudor Avădanei."

It has rained frequently over the past few days. With their personal tent sheets wrapped around their backpacks, the soldiers pitched their shelters from two sheets spread over the wet ground. Each arranged his bedding as best he could, laying down a bundle of straw, fir branches, or leafy twigs from which they shook off the rain. They slept utterly exhausted with their coats pulled tightly around them, rifles held close to their chests, and their backpacks used as pillows under their heads.

At dawn, they were roused by the sound of the bugle, drank from their mess tins a hot, dark liquid called coffee, ate a crust of bread that tasted faintly of mold, and fell back into formation to march once more.

Izu was trudging alongside Tudor, shivering in the early morning when the sun had yet to show its face and the sky threatened more rain. Road signs pointed toward Vratsa and Sofia, written in Cyrillic script, which Izu could still decipher. They followed a winding country road that rose and dipped through hills and valleys, while rocky heights loomed in the distance beneath a thick blanket of clouds.

They marched in silence, eyes fixed on the ground, skirting puddles along the way—platoons, companies, and regiments strung out in a long gray column that seemed endless. At one-point, Tudor nudged Izu with his elbow.

"Come on, Izule, say something, will you?"

"What is there to say? Better to keep quiet. Save energy…"

"But just yesterday, in that barn where we slept alongside the horses and wagons, you started telling me the story about that guy—died unknown among his own…"

"That's a long story, one that doesn't even have an ending

on so far."

"What do you mean, no ending?"

"That's how it is! It is still being fought over in court. It came to light after the man died, and a journalist came looking for him. The man, a poor kid from the back end of Călăraşi neighborhood, around the Moşi distraction park, along the gypsy quarters. No father to speak of, and one day he ran away from home - he was fifteen at the time. No one knew where he went. Years went by, and everyone forgot about him. Then, one day, he came back sick, aged, and flat broke. His relatives scolded him for mooching off their food. His mother had died, and he soon followed."

"And then what happened?" asked Tudor.

"Well, like I said, this reporter came around asking about him. The journalist had spent a long time in France and had known him there. Turns out the kid had become a stone carver."

"Who?"

"The guy! He made statues—mostly those angel ones you see in cemeteries. He was in demand, had good clients, even opened a workshop on the outskirts of Paris. A couple of apprentices lived with him, helped him with the work—and even a mistress who modeled for him. Those didn't stick around long, but he didn't care—another would take her place. But one of them got the better of him. Got him sick. When he saw there was no cure, he came back home. Didn't want to die in a foreign land."

Izu fished through his pockets for a cigarette. He would sneak a puff even in the middle of the column. After finishing the ones from his own rations, he'd take Tudor's too—Tudor had quit smoking long ago, after Vasilica's death.

"So, what did the journalist do?" Tudor asked.

"He wanted to write a book about the man's life. But back here, in the country, no one knew anything about him. Who he was or what he'd done. His relatives buried him in the paupers' cemetery. When the journalist saw that, being a God-fearing man, he decided to do a good deed. At home he had a wooden bust of the stone carver's face—made by the man himself. It wasn't finished yet, but it looked better than decent. He'd received it as a wager after a card game with the sculptor. So, he thought he'd erect a statue at the cemetery, so people could know who he had been. He hired men to build a pedestal of brick and cement, ordered a bronze plaque with his name, and when everything was ready, they planned an unveiling ceremony."

"But it didn't happen?"

"Hold on! His relatives, once they found out who the man really was—that he had a big house in Paris where his mistress now lived with their two kids—they said *that's* what matters. That the woman and kids had no right to be there, because they weren't legally recognized."

"But how could that not matter, if they were his family?"

"They said they were bastards. Don't you see? They wanted to get their hands on everything he left behind—the house, the money, the rest—claiming it was theirs by right, since *they* were family and *they* took care of him before he died. They even started fighting among themselves over who had the greater claim, who had done more for him."

"Charming family," Tudor muttered. "Upstanding folks."

"Exactly! So, when people gathered at the cemetery for the unveiling—the priest, the town officials, all the rest—guess what? The bust was missing from the pedestal."

"Where's the bust?" the journalist asked. "Who took it?"

"Well, Aunt Paulina said it had to go—that it was bringing shame to the family! 'What's that hunk of wood doing up there? You call *that* a statue?' she said. Old man Ionică took an axe to it and chopped it into kindling. 'Either you put up a proper statue,' she said, 'or nothing at all!'"

"And where's this aunt of yours now?"

"She's outside—came in a carriage. Brought her lawyer too, said: 'This doesn't smell right. That uncle's inheritance in France must be brought back *here!*""

Tudor turned his head and gave Izu a long, skeptical look, unsure whether he was telling the truth or just spinning a yarn to pass the time.

"And how do you know all this?"

"The journalist in the story—he was my mentor."

"From school?"

"No, from the paper. *Adevărul* (The Truth). He hired me when I finished high school. Took me on as an apprentice, a jack-of-all-trades. I'd carry print galleys to the press, worked in proofreading, then he had me answer readers' letters, and finally let me write reports too."

"You write for the paper now?"

"Not right now," Izu said with a grin. "Right now, I'm here—with you! But I'll write again, when there's something worth writing about. He told me I'd have to change my name, though, because in this line of work..."

Tudor turned his head to spit and blew his nose. No explanation needed—he knew fully well that Izu wouldn't make a name for himself in journalism with the name he had.

Behind them, columns of soldiers followed one after another. The men in Tudor's company marched in the same relaxed manner, keeping their distance from those ahead—some silent, lost in the swirl of their own thoughts, others chatting with the man beside them.

One of them, Petrică Buciuc—the soldier who had sharpened his pocketknife on the day of their enlistment—was walking just behind them. He felt a strange and inexplicable sense of jealousy and hostility toward Izu, seeing him always at Tudor Avădanei's side, speaking with him as if they'd known each other forever.

Not that he was truly jealous, he told himself, but this friendship needed to be broken. He couldn't quite explain why Tudor had taken up with that little Jew, always defending him if anyone said a word against him. If it hadn't been for Tudor stepping in, Izu probably wouldn't have lasted in their company.

Petrică Buciuc had reported to their platoon sergeant, Marin Salciu, that the Jew needed to be kept under surveillance—that he might be a spy. But the sergeant had taken no action.

So Buciuc spoke to a few other comrades. The men agreed to keep a close watch. If anyone noticed anything suspicious, they'd take care of the enemy—no questions asked.

What Can a Woman Do?

Princess Marie, alone at Cotroceni Palace, wrung her hands, knowing she ought to do something, yet unsure what that should be. While she had been confined to bed by phlebitis following the birth of her sixth child, Mircea, she had longed for recovery—if only to be able to contribute in some way to the war effort. And now that she was well again, now that Romanian troops had crossed into Bulgaria, she could not come to terms with the thought that no one was telling her what she was meant to do. There was war in the world, her people were facing a grave trial, Carmen Sylva is lamenting with tragical gesticulations to her audience, and she, the future queen of the country, waits idle waiting with nothing to do.

Maria recalled that there had been only one other time in her life when she had felt so close facing death, full of despair, staring blankly into nothing because she did not know how to react, what to do. Only once—and now she found herself in the same place again. She searched in vain for a way to be of use, a way to help, to contribute somehow—but no one had asked for her help, no one had offered her a chance or given her an answer.

That time had been in the summer of 1897, when Nando had fallen ill with typhoid fever. His condition was grave, and he was on the brink of death. Shaking violently with chills, his life hung by a thread after complications set in, worsened by a double pneumonia that could have taken him at any moment. Through continuous injections and round-the-clock monitoring that lasted for weeks, Doctors Ion Cantacuzino, Hristea Buicliu, and Dr. Kremnitz—a trusted friend of the royal family—took turns at his bedside day and night. In addition to them and the nurses constantly watching over him, Nando had brought with him from Germany a loyal couple— husband and wife—who had been serving him since his adolescence and cared for him with boundless devotion. These were the kind of people who would have laid down their lives for their master. They had a daughter, Mura, conceived late in life, whom they raised in the same spirit of loyalty. Mura now served as Marie's maid.

Back then, Marie was young—not yet twenty-two—and she had no knowledge of illness, for she herself had never truly been sick. She didn't know what to do. She waited helplessly, hoping for a miracle, a salvation that would restore her beloved Nando to his former self: healthy, vigorous, full of life.

Queen Elisabeth—*Aunt Elisabeth*, as Maria called her—had suffered deeply after losing her own daughter to the same illness, typhoid fever. Now, she too was overcome with memories and caught in a strange inner drama. Every detail, every dream, every gesture from the doctors, and every signs only she could interpret— was painted in the darkest shades of foreboding, marked by exclamations of despair and theatrical gestures.

Each time she climbed the stairs of Cotroceni Palace to the bedroom where Nando lay, she moved as if attending a funeral, her nose buried in a handkerchief, watching the fever-stricken young man from a distance as he raved in delirium. Then she would settle into a chair in Maria's room and begin recounting, to anyone present—even to palace servants—all the horrific scenes from her own tragic life and those of others, her beautiful hands moving dramatically, handkerchief in hand, wiping tears in a performance worthy of an ancient tragedy. Though none of this helped anyone, the scenes repeated daily throughout Nando's illness.

Maria couldn't bear to witness these pitiful displays when her own heart was breaking with fear at the thought of losing the man who was her emotional anchor, the father of her children, her Nando. In such moments, she preferred the silent company of King Carol, seated stiffly at Ferdinand's bedside, face set in stone. Like Maria, he was not one to express pain in words, gestures, or lamentation.

Watching the king, Maria tried to better understand this implacable man who had become such a heavy presence in her life— a burden almost too great to bear. She had never known constraints like the ones she now endured. She was under constant suspicion and surveillance by servants of the sovereign—placed in her service by the Grand Inquisitor herself, the queen's lady-in-waiting, along with other hostile figures ready to ascribe to her the vilest intentions, spreading false rumors that made her feel besieged by invisible forces she could not fight. None of these rumors were unknown to her uncle, because Queen Elisabeth herself, *Aunt Elisabeth,* made sure he was informed of every tale circulating about his niece.

Even so, Maria knew the king to be a just man, and she could not understand how he failed to see that she was the victim of a conspiracy meant to drag her into infamy. *"If only he could show just a little more understanding"*, she thought as she looked at the sovereign. She could not comprehend how he could be so harsh, as if he had never been young himself, as if he had never felt the need for friendship and social life—things that were as vital to her as air.

She knew he had been shaped by a military environment, where discipline and obedience to superiors were absolute. That was likely where his unyielding sense of duty had been forged, the same spirit with which he demanded that everyone around him be the same.

Nando had never tried to free himself from his uncle's dominance. But if Nando were to leave her, if he were to die, what would she do alone? With two children to care for, would she be forced to blindly obey the king's commands?

Alone, with no one to support her, how could she accept her uncle's tyranny? How could she raise her children in the way she herself had been raising in freedom, in outdoor play, without constraints that could cripple their nature and character? No. She could not accept such a fate. The blood of Albion boiled in her veins at the thought of a life like that. She had been raised in freedom, and whatever happened, her children would be raised the same. At the edge of Nando's bed, with the king seated across from her, hunched in his chair, watching his nephew struggle for breath, Maria made up her mind: *she would keep her freedom.*

In those days, crowds of people filled the courtyard of Cotroceni Palace. Day after day, they came in silence beneath the windows of the royal bedrooms, hoping for news of Nando's condition. From behind the curtains, Maria watched the outpouring of love for their prince, deeply moved the people felt and shared in the concern for their future king.

From the open windows of the adjoining room, Queen Elisabeth—her face full of sorrow—blew kisses into the air, placing her hand to her heart in gratitude, appearing before the crowd like a prima donna before the curtain. Maria, however, had the sense that many among them had come to console her, the wife of the man who was battling death, the mother of the future King of Romania. She hated the thought of Nando's death and tried to push it from her soul, but little by little, hope was wearing away, and reality forced her to confront the possibility of losing him. Even so, a deep love for those people in the palace courtyard—whose affection she felt almost humbly and could not ignore—filled her heart with an unfamiliar warmth and attachment. They were her sensitive, generous people!

And then came *that night*, the terrible night when Maria was summoned to her husband's bedside as he fought for his life. The tending nuns and doctors had given up all hope and left the final appeal to divine mercy in the hands of the priests. Throwing a robe over her nightgown, Maria entered Nando's room. He lay flat on his back, his face pale, breathing heavily, and his wide-open eyes fixed on her, as if begging for help.

When she knelt beside his bed, his hand grasped hers, and for a long time they remained like that—locked in a wordless grip that needed no speech. A priest was reciting prayers in Latin, the doctors stood defeated in a corner of the room, and Aunt Elisabeth was already convinced that the final moment had come. But Maria still hoped—she could not imagine that Nando would leave her now, when his young soul was still full of unfulfilled dreams.

Toward dawn, Ferdinand began to breathe more easily. One of the doctors came closer and took his pulse—it was stronger. A glimmer of hope lit up in his eyes, and in that moment, everyone presents, tears in their eyes, felt the need to reach for someone, for an embrace, anyone it didn't matter who, because they had all witnessed a miracle and were utterly exhausted.

The crisis had passed! The tension in King Carol's face eased, a faint smile appeared at the corner of his lips. The morning light washed over their souls, as clear as water, after the turmoil of a night that would be remembered by all who had stood around Ferdinand, praying for him. Now, the sun of hope had risen, and suddenly a new joy swept away the burdens of the night before.

The prince's convalescence was long, marked by recurring bouts of fever from the past. The doctors recommended the clean mountain air of Sinaia. Once there, he was transported on a stretcher by Mountain Hunter officers to the Foișor Castle, used by the King Carol as summer residence until Peleș Castle construction finished in 1883. Later Foișor Castle became the summer residence for Ferdinand and Maria until 1902 when The Pelișor Castel was ready for young princes living.

Prince Ferdinand was bedridden for six weeks. By the end of this period, he was unrecognizable. A long, chestnut beard had grown on his face, his hair had turned completely white, and his complexion had taken on the waxy pallor of candlelight. His eyes and cheeks had sunk deep into the bony hollows of his skull. This image would become emblematic of the man who would later become the most beloved and respected king in Romanian history.

Now, as then, Maria felt she had to do something as her conscience tormented her being left out in time of general struggle. But what? What could she do—an inexperienced woman—when all affairs of the front were entrusted to those who knew what had to be done, who were trained for such efforts and had already endured similar trials?

In such a situation, there was only one person who could help her—a friend she could trust: Prince Barbu Știrbey[xxvii]. This man, Barbu Alexandru Știrbey, always found the most fitting responses to situations that required wise counsel. He was equally cherished by the king, the queen, and the young princely couple for his quiet nature, thoughtful judgment in all matters, and reliability.

As proof of his trust, King Carol had appointed him administrator of the Royal Domains after the death of the previous administrator and the king's friend, Ioan Kalinderu. When the king chose him for this role—despite his youth—he had in mind the prince's loyalty, just like that of all his family, who had voluntarily renounced their rights to the throne at the beginning of Carol's reign as ruling prince of Romania in 1866.

Știrbey and all his kin had remained loyal to the king throughout their lives. Prince Barbu Știrbey was capable and enterprising. His past left no room for doubt about his character, honor, and devotion. The king believed that being close in age to the heirs of the throne, he could one day bring great benefit to the country through balanced advice and wise guidance.

The prince's residence was set in the heart of a vast forest, at Buftea, in a manor begun in 1850 by the former ruler of

Wallachia, Barbu Dimitrie Știrbey, and completed in 1864 by the prince's father, Alexandru Știrbey.

Among ancient trees were flower gardens, a lake with a sandy shore waiting for visitors, and even riding paths where one could gallop across long distances. Both Barbu Știrbey and three of his four daughters loved this sport, and Maria, in their company, showcased her skill in splendid horseback rides with her friends. She took great pleasure in coming here during the sweltering summer afternoons in Bucharest, and she was always welcomed with joy by Nadeja, Barbu's wife, and their daughters.

On this visit to Buftea, Maria met Elisa Brătianu[xxviii], Barbu's sister and now the wife of Ionel Brătianu, the former Prime Minister back in 1908 to 1910. Elisa had previously been married to Alexandru Marghiloman, from whom she had amicably separated, but they had remained friends. Though initially intimidated by Elisa's presence, Maria gradually grew close to her, eventually referring to her, half-jokingly, as "my stern old lady." Tall, dignified, and aristocratic by birth and education, Elisa impressed Maria deeply. Her manner, eloquence, and sincerity became a source of inspiration to her.

"I'm so happy finding you here, my stern old lay" said Maria embracing her friend.

"Why?"

"Because I'm ashamed to say, I could not find my place…"

" What do you mean?"

"Don't you see? We are in middle of a war, everyone is helping with something, and I am doing nothing."

"Well, if you really want to do something, there are ways to help…" told Elisa.

Maria then learned with great surprise that Elisa was already deeply involved in the work of the Red Cross. She was organizing hospitals for wounded soldiers—mobile medical units near the front, equipped with doctors, nurses, and supplies. It was considered the duty of the ladies of high society to see to these matters. Elisa explained that such efforts had long been expected of women in their position: managing field hospitals, ambulances, and medical care—all done independently, without state support, funded through donations and charity.

"Why has no one told me about this until now?" Maria asked.

"Because you never showed any interest in learning about it," Elisa replied.

"That's not true! I wanted to—but how was I supposed to know what you were all doing?"

Elisa fixed her with a measured, thoughtful look.

"Listen, Missy. Why don't you use your time for something more serious?"

Caught off guard, Maria could only respond in a quiet voice, "Because I'm not clever enough."

"You have no right to say such a thing!" Elisa answered sharply. "You're as intelligent as you need to be—you're just too lazy to use your mind. Try to see what you're capable of if you'd only stop giving in to idleness!"

"Me? What do I even know how to do?"

Maria had never truly believed she could be useful to anyone. No one had ever asked anything of her before.

"You can do plenty, if you put your mind to it. You could be a great help. Just try."

The Hailstorm

"This doesn't smell right to me," Izu muttered at one point. "What I'm seeing here—it's got me thinking."

"What do you mean?"

"I'm afraid we might be walking straight into a trap. We just keep marching and marching… don't you see? Nothing's happening. What if they're waiting to catch us in a valley like this and come down on us from the mountains? They wouldn't even need bullets—just boulders and rocks from up there would be enough to kill us."

"Oh, come on, quit scaring the kids with your dark thoughts! You think our generals haven't considered that? Really now? You don't think they've sent scouts ahead to figure out what's going on? What kind of journalist are you if you don't know we've even got airplanes[xxix]?"

"Airplanes? I haven't seen a single one yet."

"That doesn't matter. That engineer—what's his name—Aurel Vlaicu, he's got two planes already. He's even flown over the mountains with one. Did you know he won a prize last year at a contest in Austria? See? That's why I'm telling you—we're more advanced than people give us credit for!"

"I know that" Izu replied unhappy that he did not see the situation on that perspective. "There's another Romanian too, he built a plane in England."

"Yeah, last year. Hari, or something was his name.? Not Hari—Henri! Henri Coandă. I read he was awarded too. Italy and Romania each ordered ten of his airplanes."

Indeed, on June 17, 1910, the Romanian engineer Aurel Vlaicu unveiled his original powered monoplane, *Vlaicu I*, in Bucharest near Cotroceni. Construction began in 1909 at the Army Arsenal in Bucharest, and the flight was a success. A large crowd witnessed the event—journalists, dignitaries, and even the 17-year-old Prince Carol II.

With that flight, Romania became the third country in the world—after the United States and France—to possess a fully functioning aircraft, designed, built, and flown by a national pilot. Even more impressively, later that year Vlaicu flew a mission between Slatina and Piatra Olt, carrying an official message—demonstrating to the world the practical potential of aviation for communications.

In December 1910, Vlaicu began construction on his second flying machine, the *Vlaicu II*, with which he competed in an international aviation contest in Vienna in 1912. There, he won several awards totaling 7,500 Austro-Hungarian crowns—a fortune at the time.

Now, with the army mobilized, the Military Aeronautics Service—placed under the command of the Inspector General of Engineering—established two flight schools to support the military from the air. One of the schools had an airfield at Corabia, with five airplanes, including two Farman III models built in Chitila, and one *Vlaicu II*. On July 9, 1913, Aurel Vlaicu signed a contract with the Ministry of War, specifying that both he and his mechanic, Miron Maieraş, would serve as civilian personnel attached to the army.

The second school operated from two airfields, one at Segarcea and the other at Bechet. It had nine airplanes, including a two-seater *Bristol-Coandă* and another *Vlaicu II*. During the war, Romanian aircraft carried out photographic reconnaissance missions over Bulgaria, dropped leaflets, and—marking a historical first—flew over an enemy capital: Sofia, which was explored from the sky by hostile airplanes.

Meanwhile, Tudor, Izu, and the rest of their regiment kept marching in long columns that stretched endlessly down the road. The midday sun was blazing, and the men, now exhausted, trudged up a winding road that zigzagged along the back of a curving hill. Not a single tree, house, or living creature was in sight.

They hadn't even reached the summit when, suddenly, heavy clouds rolled in behind them, and a fierce downpour struck. The rain was joined by jagged, frozen pellets that hammered down harder than bullets on the soldiers' bodies. It came fast and furious, slamming onto their cloth caps that offered no protection. The men raised their arms above their heads like makeshift shields.

All around, the landscape was covered in a crust of ice, scattered like sand across the ground as if it had snowed. The marching columns broke apart. Caught off guard by the unexpected hailstorm, the men pressed into one another, trying to find shelter in their shared warmth, covering their heads with whatever they could find. Some lifted their knapsacks overhead for protection. In the confusion, no one thought to unroll the tarps carried wrapped around their packs for just such emergency.

Izu dropped to one knee, curling up with his head against his friend's chest, while Tudor hunched over him to shield him from the hail. All around them, water splashed violently. Then, as suddenly as it had begun, the storm stopped—like someone had flipped a switch. Not long after, the sun reappeared, just as bright and scorching as before, blazing down like a red-hot iron plate.

Everyone was soaked to the bone. Water had seeped through every layer of their clothes, all the way to their skin—even into their boots. With each step, their feet, wrapped in coarse cloth bandages, squelched loudly inside their soaked footwear.

"Damn that rain! Just what we needed right now!" Tudor

burst out, letting off steam.

With their ranks scattered, the soldiers were now spread out along the roadside. Each one stared helplessly at his own miserable state, unsure what to do in clothes that clung to their bodies like icy compresses. Izu checked the pocket where he kept his cigarettes. When he reached in, all he found were damp, unraveling shreds of tobacco.

"Yours are just as soaked, huh?" he asked Tudor.

Tudor nodded, then slung his rucksack back over his shoulder and said:

"Come on. We can't just stand here. I think we've still got 15 or 20 kilometers to go before we reach the overnight camp."

Izu nodded and followed. Other soldiers trailed behind them, scattered along the road, looking like peas spilled from a split sack— the storm had shaken them loose and scattered them.

Suddenly, as they trudged along like a herd without a shepherd, a company caught up to them, marching in tight formation. The rhythmic stomp of their boots was matched by the voices of the marching men, singing in unison:

March on, march on, drum is loud,

March strong, hearts and heads held proud!

With packs strapped tight upon backs,

Rifles ready for attacks.

Hurrah!

Be it sun or skies of gray,

Be it snow or rainy day,

Through storm chills, through mud or dust—

We march forward, for we must!

Tudor and the others stepped aside to let the column pass, watching them parade by in step. Then, energized by the spirit of the marching song, they fell in behind, picking up the same cadence, as if the enthusiasm of the singing soldiers had sparked a second wind in them.

The water had quickly dried from the road and nearby fields, and under the strong summer sun, steam began to rise from the soldiers' bodies and uniforms as they started to dry after the downpour. One by one, the troops emerged from behind to rejoin their companies, and soon the columns reformed, marching again to the steady cadence of singing voices.

A young officer on horseback came by to inspect the

formation and asked the company's platoon leader, Marin Salciu, if everything was in order. A soldier stepped out of the column to request permission from the commander.

"Wait until the next rest stop."

"I can't, sir! My stomach hurts badly".

"Alright, go ahead—but when you return, report to the platoon leader. Understood?"

"Yes, sir!" the soldier replied, hurrying off into the bushes.

Seeing the soldier duck into the brush, Petrică Buciuc nudged the comrade beside him with his elbow.

"Was that the Jew who went into the bushes?"

"I don't know, I didn't look at him," the man answered.

They rested on the edge of a village, where each soldier rummaged through his ration sack for the cold meal prepared for the road—dry field bread in the form of hard biscuits, canned food, and maybe a piece of fruit saved from dinner or picked along the way.

After eating, Izu pointed out a cherry plum tree at the head of the village yard, heavy with ripened fruit. Someone had already shaken it, and golden plums lay scattered across the ground. Tudor and Izu filled their caps with fruit, their rifles slung over their shoulders and wandered nearby. At the back of the yard stood a small cottage with whitewashed walls and a thatched roof, its door wide open. Inside, on a bench by the clay oven, an elderly woman lay collapsed, her face sunken, surrounded by the stench and mess of vomit, completely unattended. She mumbled, motioning weakly for water, but no one dared to go near.

From the doorway, Tudor hesitated—torn between pity and caution—wondering whether to help. But Izu pulled him away:

"I heard cholera's been going around here…"

The First Stop

The Romanian cavalry halted near Orhanie, about 40 kilometers from Sofia, on July 12, 1913. General Averescu established the army's general headquarters there, and Prince Ferdinand sent word to the King in Sinaia about the new situation. King Carol's order came swiftly: *"Romanian troops are not to enter Sofia!"*

At the news of this order, every soldier and officer felt a deep sense of disappointment, a sentiment shared at home as well, by both the politicians in government and the general public. King Carol, however, was determined not to humiliate his adversary, the Tsar of Bulgaria, Ferdinand I, who was soon to arrive in Sinaia, where he was typically hosted at Peleş Castle. The Romanian sovereign was not especially pleased about this visit, for the Bulgarian ruler was known for his frivolous manner, his fondness for parties, and a certain air of superiority he displayed toward others.

After losing all its European territories except for Adrianople—and with them, its prestige as a major European power—Turkey entered the war on July 12, 1913, attacking Bulgaria in a bid for revenge and perhaps to salvage some measure of victory. Surrounded, Bulgaria soon realized it could not continue the fight against enemies advancing from every direction, and on

July 13, 1913, it litigated for peace.

The armistice with Romania was signed on July 22, while hostilities with the other states continued until July 31. Although not a single shot had been fired on enemy soil, another far more dreadful enemy had made its appearance: *cholera*[xxx].

The first case of cholera in the Romanian army was identified on July 13, 1913, in Vrața. That same day, Dr. Victor Babeș recorded another case in Fernandovo. It was already known that after the First Balkan War, cases of cholera had been detected in Bulgaria and Serbia. In Greece, the epidemic had been less severe, since the population there had been vaccinated. But in Bulgaria, preventive measures against the epidemic were virtually nonexistent. Military and prisoner camps were often established near populated areas, and outbreaks of cholera spread rapidly.

In their retreat from the enemy, the Bulgarian army had thrown human and animal corpses into wells and rivers instead of burying them. Unaware of the danger, Romanian and Serbian soldiers drank from these wells, bathed in the rivers, washed their clothes there, and used equipment found in Bulgarian-evacuated garrisons—equipment that may have been contaminated. Many cases of cholera in the army were misdiagnosed by some doctors as typhoid fever. Even worse, the field hospitals and ambulances had been equipped only to treat wounded soldiers (who were essentially nonexistent on this front) and were therefore useless in combating digestive illnesses. There were no doctors trained in the prevention and treatment of infectious diseases, and no medicines to help them.

Three days after the first cholera cases were identified, on July 16, the 1st Army Corps had already recorded 16 deaths, 64 seriously ill patients, and over 200 suspected cases of infection. In the 2nd Army Corps, on the same day, there were three deaths, 15 critically ill, and 40 suspected cases. The situation was dire. Alarm spread through the ranks, and when Dr. Mihail Manicatide, a close disciple of the renowned scientist Victor Babeş, alerted his superiors that cholera was the dominant epidemic in Bulgaria and that preventive vaccination of troops must be implemented, he was met with vague assurances that it was a "military secret."

Another military doctor, Constantin Argentoianu, fought against the negligence and indifference of some commanding officers—among them, General Crăiniceanu, who avoided contact with the troops but had ordered a private latrine to be built on stilts for his exclusive use. Under his command, the troops suffered more than any other unit. At the same time, some civil and sanitary authorities in Romania misinformed the public for entirely political reasons.

At a cavalry regiment stationed about ten kilometers from Orhanie, an army doctor discovered that a well in the center of the camp was contaminated and warned the commanding officer not to use the water. The officer mockingly dismissed the warning, filled a mug with water from the well, and drank it. Three days later, he died in excruciating agony.

On July 19, the mayor of Bucharest announced the closure of the border with Bulgaria, and the next day, July 20, the newspapers *Adevărul* and *Opinia* published reports on the situation in Bulgaria, stating that 2,128 cases of cholera had been confirmed in the Romanian army, along with 223 deaths.

Father Brumuşescu, attached to the 14th Artillery Regiment, recalled in his notes:

"We arrived late at night in Orhanie, in pitch-black darkness. We camped on the western side of the town, near the Bulgarian barracks, where Turkish prisoners had died of cholera. Our soldiers, utterly exhausted, and unable to see anything in the darkness, gathered the straw they found lying around to make bedding, and fell asleep instantly—without realizing they were sleeping in the bed of death. The next day, in the daylight, the filth of the place and the condition of the straw revealed that these were the beds used by cholera-stricken Turks."

In the newspaper *Viaţa*, a military doctor wrote: "On July 14, more and more sick men continued to arrive. At eight in the morning, I set out with a colleague to inspect the patients in the hospitals of Orhanie. They were placed in a large room inside the barracks, which had not been cleaned. There were no beds. The men lay on the floor, still in uniform, their faces sunken and bluish, their bodies emaciated, fingers shriveled. Most could barely moan or ask for water, some were delirious, their arms and hands twitching with spasm. They vomited on the floorboards, relieved themselves there too. There was nothing for their care—not even containers for water. I have seen much misery, but nothing as harrowing as this. There were seventy-seven patients; five had already died. The army corps ambulance had arrived and, together with the chief physician of the 1st Corps, was trying to organize a hospital. But the lack of furniture, containers, linens, medical instruments, medicine—even antiseptics— made the presence of doctors futile."

A few hospitals for the care of the sick were hastily organized in the south of the Danube, including one that was opened in Orhanie. On July 16, the Red Cross sent a mobile hospital and 200 beds to Teliş, in Bulgaria. Elisa Brătianu, acting on her own initiative, took command of a mobile ambulance and opened a hospital with 180 beds.

Once the epidemic broke out, the military authorities, under the command of Prince Ferdinand, supported the sanitary authorities throughout the campaign to fight the disease, doing everything that was humanly possible. The civil health service, led by Dr. Mina Minovici, contributed everything at its disposal.

DOMNIȚA AND TUDOR AVĂDANEI

On July 17, 1913, Lieutenant Doctor Ion Cantacuzino was promoted to the rank of Major Doctor and appointed Inspector General of the Sanitary Service Directorate within the Romanian Army's General Headquarters. Aware of the gravity of his mission, the new Inspector General set out with a team of doctors to inspect all army hospitals in Bulgaria and along the Romanian side of the Danube.

Prince Ferdinand maintained a central command post and communication hub with all military divisions in Bulgarian territory, accompanied by the General Staff. Alongside him was Prince Carol II, who, at 19, had become a handsome, intelligent, and energetic young man. Also, present were General Alexandru Averescu, General Physician Mihai Călinescu, and other high-ranking army officers.

After completing their inspection of the military detachments stationed in Bulgaria, Dr. Cantacuzino's team took part in a high-level meeting with the army leadership, presenting their findings.

The doctors' conclusions were not encouraging. Multiple deviations from the given instructions had been committed, and because of that, it was impossible to predict when and at what cost the epidemic would be brought under control. Strict and general measures had to be taken to ensure no infected soldier would carry the disease back to Romania upon the army's return.

All those present at the meeting listened silently as Dr. Cantacuzino explained the situation.

"I don't understand—what exactly was done that shouldn't have been?" asked the Chief of the General Staff, General Averescu.

"The most important thing, General. We knew—and you were informed—that cholera was rampant in Bulgaria. Yet no one imagined an epidemic among our own troops was even possible. Our medical units were unprepared to face it. The army crossed the border without being vaccinated against cholera, even though we had enough vaccine for every soldier.

The doctors were not trained to combat an epidemic, and the necessary medicines were not distributed to the medical units."

"But where did this cholera even come from?" asked Prince Ferdinand.

"Let me first tell you what a Russian doctor said. He mentioned that they had a tough time with this disease during the Russo-Japanese War of 1905. He said, *'War is an epidemic of the wounded and a breeding ground for epidemics.'* Colonel Cihoski, attached to the Serbian General Headquarters, who studied the origins of the cholera outbreak in the First Balkan War, believes the disease was transmitted by Turks from Anatolia, from whom the

Bulgarians became infected during the Battle of Çatalca. We've seen with our own eyes how poor sanitary conditions are in Bulgarian villages. They set up prisoner-of-war camps for Turkish captives around the central villages of Bulgaria. That's how cholera spread to the Serbs, and now it has reached us. Do you know what that scoundrel General Nikola Ivanov did during their retreat from the Serbs? He gave the order to throw the bodies of cholera victims—humans and animals alike—into wells and rivers. Isn't that a crime against humanity?"

"What do you propose?" asked General Averescu again.

"It's a complicated situation. We have a cholera vaccine, and it must be administered to the entire military and civilian personnel. In Orhanie, we must halt the entry of any more military units because that's where the highest number of cases are. Soldiers must be supplied with soap to wash their hands frequently and maintain proper hygiene. Latrines must be relocated far from the mobile kitchens and covered daily with earth. Eating raw fruits and vegetables should be strictly forbidden, as should visiting the sick in hospitals. Water is a major concern—it must be boiled before consumption. Bathing in rivers and lakes should only be allowed after the water has been tested."

"How do we prevent bringing the disease back into the country?"

"That's the most pressing issue. I already mentioned vaccinating the soldiers.

First, we must set up quarantine zones for everyone—even those who appear healthy.

Five days—that's the incubation period for the disease. During those five days, no one should cross into Romania without staying in quarantine to ensure they're not carrying the infection.

Anyone with a fever must be separated from the healthy and kept under medical supervision until they recover or pass through the illness. Even those without any symptoms should undergo quarantine. All this needs to happen before the troops return to their garrisons.
Otherwise, we won't be able to stop cholera from spreading. But first of all, in Orhanie, we need to start vaccinating every soldier, officer, and commander in every unit."

After the conference, 50,000 soldiers stationed at Orhanie began receiving the first dose of the anti-cholera vaccine on July 21, 1913. The next doses were scheduled to be administered on July 27 and August 3.

Visiting the Sick

After her conversation in Buftea with Elisa Brătianu, attended also by Barbu Știrbey, Maria began to look more closely at the situation—especially the fact that across the Danube, cholera cases had broken out in the Romanian army. She also learned that King Carol had forbidden any civilian from crossing the Danube. Elisa's words echoed clearly in the princess's mind:

"You could be of great help. Try!"

"I could be of help. But how? Sitting idly, I can be of no help at all!"

She decided to visit the patients in the Red Cross hospitals that were set up along the Danube. These visits terrified Maria, who had never imagined the extent of suffering endured by those stricken with cholera. Never before had she felt such pity, such a newly awakened desire to help her ailing soldiers. From that point on, she knew she had an important role to play in the fight against the disease. More than anyone, it was her duty to lead those who wished to improve the situation. She had to act—even at the cost of her own life—for she too could become the next victim.

At the same time, she felt something shift within her, a mysterious mechanism turning on and altering the course of her life.

She could no longer be the same person she had been before. All her past carelessness and frivolity no longer belonged to her. Now, these children lying in their beds were like her own children, they *were* her children. They were her people, and it was her duty to care for them. As she traveled from hospital to hospital, Maria's horror grew—not only because of the ravages of the disease, but also due to the way hospitals were being managed.

When she heard that there were hospitals on the opposite bank of the Danube, in Bulgaria, Maria defied the king's order and crossed in secret to see what was happening there. The sight that awaited her was even more terrifying. In a nearly deserted village, abandoned by the fear of the spreading epidemic, Maria found a hospital where many Romanian soldiers had been nearly forgotten, on the verge of death for lack of doctors and medicine. She stared, horrified and disheartened, realizing that even there the hospitals were equipped to treat wounds—but no other illnesses, and certainly not an epidemic as virulent as cholera. Everything was lacking: nurses, doctors, medicine, and more.

Without any concern for her own health, Maria dashed through every corner of the place and immediately realized what was missing most: a leader. Someone with full authority who could uplift spirits without showing panic, without complaining—someone with a calm face and a clear mind.

Meeting with Dr. Ion Cantacuzino and his assistant, Dr. Alexandru Slătineanu—both on an inspection tour—Maria saw that they too were appalled by the negligence and disorder in those death-houses called hospitals. She held a long meeting with them and came to understand that she alone, because of her unique position, had the authority to be heard by everyone, civilians, officers, or reservists alike. She had the power to intervene with suggestions, to organize, to make decisions, and to give orders to resolve the problem at hand.

Without hesitation, Maria returned quickly to Sinaia to discuss what she had seen with her uncle. The king listened silently as she presented her case, describing the dire conditions in the hospitals and how necessary her presence was in coordinating efforts to care for the sick.

"Our troops are stationed in Bulgaria," the king said. "Greece and Serbia have not yet signed the armistice, and we're preparing for the peace conference in Bucharest. I agree that you should prepare the hospital at Zimnicea before the troops return from Bulgaria, because there will be many sick men, and we must not allow the disease to spread into our country. There is much work to do, and before they arrive, you'll have time to gather the necessary personnel, arrange accommodation, set up the hospital, acquire medicine, prepare for disinfection, and everything else. At the same time, don't forget to take care of yourself. You have children—and a great responsibility in this country. Be prudent in what you do. Don't try to do everything on your own. Remember that you're surrounded by doctors and specialists who know more than you do, and that your mission is to facilitate, not to get in the way. Go with God, Missy! May the Lord be with you!"

In Front of the Tent

Tudor's company had been stationed for about three days somewhere roughly 30 kilometers from Sofia, upstream from a village on the edge of which flowed a clear, winding stream. The company kitchen used its waters for cooking and washing. Tudor's comrades were on duty, helping clean mess kits and perform other chores. The latrines had to be tended to daily with new pits dug, old ones filled with earth or disinfected with slaked lime.

Supplies arrived in wagons covered with canvas, pulled all the way by scrawny horses. As with most provisions, the bread often arrived moldy and underbaked in the middle. Other food wasn't in much better shape. The onions and potatoes were spoiled, their tubers sprouting greenish, octopus-like tendrils. The cornmeal was rancid, and the meat had an unpleasant smell.

After nightfall, there was an order not to light fires in front of the tents—but since the fighting had stopped, no one paid much attention to it anymore. The nights were cold, and many fell ill because of it. Some started having stomach troubles, diarrhea, chills, and fevers. There was no doctor in the company, just an ambulance driven by a chauffeur and staffed by a single nurse who came to check on the sick and distribute medicine. More serious cases were transported to a field hospital using the same covered wagons that had brought bread from the homeland. As the illness spread among the soldiers, fear began to take hold of everyone. Half-joking, half-serious, some said the horses were better cared for, since they at least had veterinarians.

After dinner, Tudor sat on a boulder in front of his tent under the evening sun. He took a postcard and pencil from his pack and began to write home:

Dear Father,

I kiss your hand! I don't know what things are like back in the village, but here, although we're at peace, it's not good. They say many have cholera—even among us, in the army. It's said this disease spares no one and cuts down many lives. There've been a few cases in our regiment too. I saw them taking the sick to the hospital in the same wagons they brought our provisions in. Next to those lying on stretchers, they also put men who'd just developed a fever. For now, we don't know what's going to happen, because we're stuck here waiting to be sent home.

We're all quite worried about the disease, and many say they'd have preferred death by bullets in battle over the slow agony of fearing a sickness that spreads from one man to another like mange. We now have orders to drink boiled tea three times a day instead of water. We're only allowed to drink boiled water.

My comrade, a Jew, got word from his family that the

disease has reached Bucharest too. We heard that peace negotiations have begun. Is it true? No one knows anything here, and we're all eager to return home. I'll write again another time, because now it's dark and I can't see what I'm writing anymore.

Tell Mother Priestess I kiss her hand and wish her good health! The same to you!

Stay well!

Tudor Avădanei.

After he finished writing, Tudor went to drop the postcard in the mailbag bound for home. The sun had long since set, and the cold was beginning to creep in. Shivering, he thought he might warm up by making a round among his comrades. Near the bivouac, where the food was being prepared, he found a group of soldiers deep in conversation. Among them, he spotted Izu talking animatedly with Sergeant Salciu and Lieutenant Radu Roşianu. Tudor stopped a short distance from the group.

"It's true that the men are worried about the disease and worn out from waiting for the withdrawal orders," said the sergeant, "but what can we do? These things are out of our hands!"

"I think we *can* help them forget the sickness and their troubles," said Izu. "We can cheer them up. The men need a little encouragement…"

"What do you mean?" asked the lieutenant.

"Well, everyone here knows a joke, a poem, a ballad, or a song. Our evenings are free. We could organize a gathering—an evening of stories and songs, maybe even a football match or some wrestling. It would do a lot to lift morale…"

"What the soldier is saying makes sense." Lieutenant Roşianu showed his agreement. "I'll ask Captain Petrescu for permission. But in the meantime, someone should go around and make a list of those willing to perform."

"I could do that!" Izu offered eagerly. "We might even find some musical instruments in the village. There are people around here who understand Romanian."

"How do you know that?" asked Sergeant Marin Sălciu.

"I went into the village looking for something to eat—I was hungry. I stepped into a yard and asked if they'd sell me something. The man said he had some eggs and had his wife fry them up. He welcomed me into their home and gave me bread and cheese. He told me his ancestors were Romanians who had come over the frozen Danube with their sheep to pasture in this region. There are others like them in the village. He didn't even let me pay."

"Well, how about that!" Lieutenant Roşianu exclaimed in

surprise.

"They admire us," Izu went on. "He said we freed them from the Turks in '77, and this time we brought peace—peace that stopped the bloodshed between brothers. He said we hadn't touched their daughters or their homes."

"Yes, but who gave you permission to leave camp and go into the village?" the sergeant cut in.

"I wasn't the only one there. A lot of soldiers from our company went into the village during their free time," Izu replied.

"Maybe *they* had permission, but you didn't come to me for approval. Who else went with you?"

"No one. I went alone."

"And who else did you meet on the way?"

"No one. Like I said, there were other soldiers in the village streets, but I walked there by myself."

"From now on, you don't leave the bivouac without informing me," the sergeant ordered. "And never alone. Understood?"

Stunned by the sudden change in tone, Izu snapped to attention before his superior and answered bitterly:

"Understood."

Lieutenant Roşianu, visibly confused, pulled the sergeant aside by the sleeve:

"What's all this? What do you have against him?"

"Sir, don't you know? He's a Jew. The others suspect him of being a traitor."

"On what grounds?"

"Well, don't you see? He's a Jew."

Tudor had been watching the exchange but said nothing. Izu came to stand beside him in silence. The group dispersed quietly, each returning to their own corner of the camp. The moon drifted silently above the mountain ridges.

Zimnicea

After her meeting with King Carol, Maria returned to Bucharest. She was pleased that the sovereign had not rejected her request to care for the sick, but she also knew that a great responsibility now rested on her shoulders. She sat down in her study at Cotroceni, took a notepad, and began writing down her goals, and people who might help her achieve them. Telephone lines had recently been installed between Bucharest and Sinaia, and there were already a few subscribers in the capital. She called Elisa Brătianu to share the news.

"Bravo, Missy! I'm happy for you!" came her friend's reply. "What do you plan to do?"

"I need help. I want to mobilize a few trustworthy people to assist me there, because I won't be able to be everywhere at once. I'll need material support—beds, bedding, bandages, and all sorts of supplies that will need to be constantly replenished depending on the number of patients. And God knows what else I'll need before this is over..."

"You're right, Missy! You already know what the situation in Zimnicea is like—you've been there. I imagine that little hospital will have to be expanded, because there'll be more patients than anyone planned for when it was established. Don't forget to reach out to the authorities for help, and the Red Cross. Some of our acquaintances have already fled abroad for fear of cholera. And don't forget—if there's anything I can do, I'm here to help. Don't leave me out."

"How could I leave you out, my stern old lady?" Maria replied with a laugh, then hung up the phone.

She pulled a sheet of personal stationery from her desk drawer and began writing the first letter. She didn't go to bed until she had finished a whole stack of letters to be sent out the next morning to various destinations.

When she arrived at the hospital camp in Zimnicea, Maria was accompanied by her lady-in-waiting, Mrs. Mavrodi—a calm and kind woman—and by Elena Perticari, a deeply modest friend and the daughter of Dr. Carol Davila. Like her father, Elena was full of patriotism, and although she had a fragile constitution, she had insisted on joining this field of suffering, ready to sacrifice herself by doing whatever work was needed.

Also with Maria was her young maid, Mura, the daughter of Nando's German servants, who still worked at Cotroceni. Shy and eager to fulfill the princess' every wish, Mura had become a close and indispensable companion to Maria, a confidante of her thoughts and, at the same time, the executor of all those little duties that ensured the princess appeared radiant and impeccable in public each day. Each of them was fully aware of the risk they were taking by following Maria into this camp of illness, but they had bravely agreed to join the nurses, orderlies, and doctors, and to carry out, in silence, whatever was asked of them—at any time, day or night.

Maria herself could hardly believe that her appeals to the authorities and to her friends would be answered so quickly. And yet, everyone responded with enthusiasm, offering whatever they could, and thanks to them, supplies soon began arriving in Zimnicea. Authorities, institutions, and members of high society all contributed to the collection of goods and provisions so desperately needed by the sick in the military camps. Medicines, bandages, blankets, sheets, and changes of clothing began arriving almost daily. Treats such as chocolate, cigarettes, and other comforts came in sufficient quantities that Maria could give the patients she visited not only the consolation of a kind word, but also the joy of receiving gifts from home, a sign that they had not been forgotten. Each time she appeared among the sick, her presence was received with the joy one feels upon seeing a unique being—almost reverently, like an angel with a mother's tenderness, or a saint.

The Peace of Bucharest was signed on August 10, 1913—celebrated with twenty-one cannon salutes at 10 o'clock in the morning. Prince Carol II, who had accompanied his father during the campaign in Bulgaria, was embodied the cheerfulness of a young man full of intelligence and ready for any responsibility. Having inherited much of his mother's charm, he was proud that she had been entrusted with the supervision of the hospital in Zimnicea and wanting to be of help, he requested a transfer there and joined her.

The evacuation of the occupation troops from Bulgarian territory was to be completed within fifteen days, following the demilitarization of the Bulgarian army. It was expected that the return of several hundred thousand Romanian soldiers to the country would place great strain on the efforts to fight cholera in the hospitals along the Danube.

Though happy to have him by her side as her right hand—because Maria knew she could rely on her son's ability to carry out any task she might give him—she was nonetheless terribly worried to see him in that lion's den, where death was cutting down men as young and full of promise as he was. What could she say to him? How could she make him understand that he had to be careful, that he was the hope of the entire nation, its future? How could she convince him that if anyone needed to be protected, he was the very first who should not be exposed? And yet, at the same time, she was proud that her own son was fearless, that he had the courage to get involved without hesitation, and that he burned with the same desire as she did—to be of service.

Soon, he would become an indispensable helper to her,

alongside her lady-in-waiting, Mavrodi, and the daughter of Dr. Carol Davila—Elena, the wife of General Perticari.

In such a demanding mission as the one she had taken on, Maria needed people who were ready to face any situation without regard for themselves. That is why she turned to Sister Pucci[xxxi], the Mother Superior of the nuns from the Order of Saint Vincent de Paul in Bucharest, whom she had known for some time. At the princess's urging, Sister Pucci—originally from Italy—responded immediately, bringing with her a group of hardworking nuns and sisters of charity, for whom no labor or hardship was too great, and no exhaustion seemed to slow the zeal with which they worked. Maria provided them with a large tent in the middle of the camp, and they began their work at once, without complaints or concern for the harsh and inadequate conditions under which they were asked to serve.

Meanwhile in Bucharest, another prominent figure from a family that had given the country notable rulers and ministers—Vladimir Ghica[xxxii]—had recently returned from an apostolic journey through many countries of the world. He devoted himself to charitable work, opening the country's first free clinic. At the same time, he organized and laid the foundations for the first Catholic hospital and sanatorium in Romania—Saint Vincent de Paul, a charitable institution. Maria also turned to the services of this saintly man, who joined the cholera camp in Zimnicea as a humble orderly. He chose to work in the tent assigned to the most unfortunate patients, those beyond hope of recovery, a place grimly known as "Hell." There, this lay prince of the Gospel labored like a true missionary, tending to both the physical and spiritual needs of the suffering, offering his service for the most grueling shift—night duty. Although he himself was in frail health, he survived the cholera outbreak of 1913—but not the wave of Communist terror four decades later. He died, beaten and tortured, in Jilava prison on May 16, 1953. For his life of sacrifice and virtue, Prince Ghica was canonized in 2013.

Not everyone welcomed Princess Maria and the members of her entourage to the lazaretto with open arms. Among the doctors, there were some who were displeased by her arrival, considering her a hindrance to their efforts in treating the afflicted—especially in a place where the lack of medical personnel was so acutely felt, and no one had time to deal with well-meaning amateurs who might interfere with their work. Before long, however, most of them began to see that the princess had no intention of interfering in the work of doctors or medical staff. On the contrary, she facilitated their efforts through better organization, the supply of medicine, and improvements to patient conditions. Each day, new problems were brought to her attention—problems that required immediate resolution, but instead of diminishing, their number kept growing.

One of the most pressing issues was the need to isolate those still going through the illness from those who hadn't contracted it or had already recovered and were soon to be returned to their garrisons. At the same time, the horror she witnessed daily made a deep impression on Maria, forcing her to summon all her strength to keep from showing the exhaustion and despair she was constantly battling. She directed all her energy toward encouraging others, maintaining an outward display of calm and optimism. In doing so, she won the admiration of everyone—doctors, orderlies, soldiers, and nurses—for never showing fatigue, hesitation, or discouragement.

But the conditions continued to worsen. The camp was far from any urban center and surrounded by rutted, muddy roads that further slowed the delivery of essential supplies. Nature itself was relentless: terrible heat alternated with heavy tropical-like rains. At times, the camp turned into a soggy morass through which Maria could barely move, even in her riding boots. When the mud dried under the scorching sun, a dreadful stench filled the air. Patients lay in large tents or crude barracks, often on straw pallets, since there weren't enough beds. Cramped tightly together with only narrow, muddy paths in between, it was nearly impossible to maintain any semblance of cleanliness. Light was scarce where it was most needed, and the atmosphere was either stifling or clammy depending on the weather.

At one end of the camp, Dr. Ion Cantacuzino had set up a makeshift laboratory, where some of his most valued students—including the Ciucă brothers—worked day and night preparing serums, vaccines, and conducting essential analyses throughout the epidemic. Realizing that they, too, needed occasional encouragement, Maria would sometimes stop by for a brief visit, careful not to disturb their work or take up their time.

One of her most invaluable supporters was Colonel Rujinski, the commander of the troops, who, along with her son Carol, worked diligently to help solve many of the camp's pressing problems.

Maria continued to visit the sick each day, speaking with them and trying to temper their yearning to return home to the fields they'd left untilled. Some, at their impatience, would have brought the illness back with them. The men listened and understood, because they knew her. They knew her from the moment they'd marched across the pontoon bridge over the Danube, where she had waited for hours with her arms full of flowers, offering one to each soldier as a token to welcome them home.

Each day, Maria received a truckload of fresh flowers from Sinaia, which she handed to the arriving troops or the sick in the camp. This was made possible thanks to the arrival of the automobile at the turn of the century, which shortened travel distances and made transport less dependent on the limitations of the railway. One of the government's first measures at the start of the Bulgarian campaign had been to requisition trucks from civilians, converting them into auxiliary vehicles or military ambulances.

At the end of the day, worn out from her visits, errands, and consultations with the staff, Maria would go to see Sister Superior Pucci in her tent. She did this whenever she needed advice, guidance, or simply a moment of calm. Petite and slender, always busy with something, Sister Pucci had become as essential to her as a mother—offering the soothing peace of a warm and nurturing spirit. Amid the rows of camp beds, the two women would sit together on overturned crates, sharing with each other the day's burdens. Sometimes Maria would find Sister Pucci tending to a pair of scrawny chickens—little more than skin and bone—on a smoky camp stove, cooking up a broth meant to warm the doctors' spirits more than their bodies. On rainy days, the wiry old nun would dart barefoot from one patient to another, through thick, ankle-deep mud. But now, both utterly exhausted, they sat face to face, waiting for water to boil for tea, something to soothe their weary souls.

"Do you know what I did today, Mother?"

"I don't. What did you do?"

"I took Mura with me this morning in the truck loaded with flowers. Our barracks are so sad and dreary. The walls are dull crimson, the light is dim, and the sun barely finds its way inside.

Even the smallest flower would bring them a little life. When we entered the ward carrying bouquets, the boys' faces lit up. It was as if we had brought them light itself. How strange these people are—so sensitive to nature, to flowers! I don't know any other people like that."

"It's true," Pucci nodded. "They love nature and everything around them…"

"I knew new troops were returning from Bulgaria today, so I went to meet them at the bridge. I gave each one a flower. Mura kept bringing me armfuls from the truck. You should've seen how happy they were! When they touched Romanian soil, many of them dropped to the ground to kiss it. I had tears in my eyes…"

"God bless you, my dear," said the nun gently. "Only a pure heart like yours could be moved by such beauty. Drink this tea—it will warm you."

Maria took the cup—a thick clay mug, painted with white chamomile flowers—and brought it to her lips. The old nun drank from a battered mess tin.

"The poor soldiers didn't know they had to stay in quarantine with us before being allowed to return to their regiments," Maria added, her tone sorrowful.

Just then, Prince Carol II appeared, dressed in civilian

clothes, a trench coat and a leather aviator's cap, the goggles pushed up onto his forehead, the straps hanging loose.

"Ah, I thought I'd find you here!" he said, kissing his mother on the cheek.

Then, spotting Sister Pucci preparing to head out to visit a patient, he greeted her warmly:

"Blessings, Sister!"

"Good thing you're here!" Maria said. "Tell us, what's the news?" she asked, motioning for him to take a seat across from her.

"Oh, a lot has happened! Marta Bibescu hosted a charity soirée for the soldiers and loaded my car with gifts and treats, which I brought there. Constance, Doctor Cantacuzino's sister, after returning from Bulgaria where she cared for the sick, has built—entirely at her own expense—a hospital for cholera patients on this side of the Danube, not far from here. She wants to transfer the more serious cases there. Grandfather's peace in Bucharest has been an international success—everyone is talking about it. First, the treaty was concluded without the intervention of the great powers. Can you imagine it?" asked Carol. "It radically redrew the map of Europe, created a new independent state—Albania—right in the middle of the continent, and, for the first time in hundreds of years, the negotiations were completed without the participation of the Ottoman Empire. Prime Minister Titu Maiorescu shone as a diplomat, Romania's prestige has grown in the eyes of other nations, and our territory expanded with the addition of the Cadrilater. I also heard that Aurel Vlaicu is working on a new aircraft—Vlaicu III—commissioned by the Marconi Radio Company. Take Ionescu told me this story and shared a funny anecdote: When they were building the Vlaicu II, they needed to measure the tension of the cables connecting the wings with a special French instrument, but it hadn't arrived yet. Everyone was in despair, time was slipping away, and they couldn't move forward. Among the soldiers nearby, there was a young Gipsy boy who played the cimbalom. What did he do? He walked past the Vlaicu I, plucked a cable and listened to the sound, then he did the same with another one on the opposite side, and finally tuned the cables on the Vlaicu II by ear, using a tuning key. When the French instrument finally arrived, it turned out the boy's tuning was perfect. What do you think of that?"

"Oh! Very interesting!"

"Yes, I thought it was amusing too… But I forgot to tell you: The king has tasked Take Ionescu with convincing the great powers to offer the throne of Albania to Aunt Elisabeth's nephew, Prince of Wied. The minister is very enthusiastic about the mission."

Maria smiled. She recognized that now, in his later years, the king was more easily swayed by his wife's suggestions. She was about to make a comment when Mura burst into the tent, visibly eager to deliver news to the princess:

"Ma'am, Mr. Tudor from Copăceni has been brought here…"

"How do you know?"

"I was there when the ambulance arrived. He was lying on a stretcher. They took him to Monsignor Ghica's barrack, where the serious cases go. I didn't recognize him at first, but I saw the silver icon medallion around his neck and ran straight here to tell you."

The Insult

Despite all the precautionary measures taken, large units passed through Zimnicea on their way to garrisons in the country without being examined, without receiving a single vaccine, contrary to regulations requiring at least two doses of anti-cholera serum. All these facts were included in a report by Colonel A. Referendaru[xxxiii], dated August 22, 1913, and submitted to King Carol I, who ordered an inspection of the troops commanded by General Hârjeu.

The orders could not have been clearer: after the peace treaty was signed in Bucharest on August 10, the evacuation of Romanian troops from Bulgarian territory was to take place between August 17 and 28, 1913—dates scheduled by the General Staff in coordination with doctors Ion Cantacuzino and Victor Babeş. Once back on the northern bank of the Danube, the military units were to be concentrated in various sectors between Zimnicea and Turnu Măgurele, where the sick were to be separated from the healthy and admitted to hospitals on the Romanian side. Troops who had received two rounds of vaccination could be dispatched to their garrisons inside the country.

Colonel Referendaru's report proposed setting up a hospital in Zimnicea for cholera patients and concentrating them there, as well as in Turnu Măgurele and Corabia, in order to vaccinate all personnel and isolate the sick and suspected cases. Another report—more of a complaint, really—came from Elisa, the wife of Ioan I. C. Brătianu, who informed the king on August 19 that cholera patients had been left unfed for three days in Turnu Măgurele. As a result of these reports, King Carol I decided to personally inspect the situation in Turnu Măgurele and Zimnicea on August 28–29.

The soldiers' return home became a source of deep anguish. When they had departed, they had been celebrated and accompanied with brass bands and patriotic songs by cheering crowds right up to the moment they crossed the Danube. But now, instead of a warm welcome, they were met with fear and suspicion at every turn. People, including their own family members, looked at them with mistrust and avoided getting too close.

In Bucharest and across the country, newspapers were publishing articles and reports from across the Danube, while also circulating all kinds of advice for preventing the spread of the epidemic. Many journalists rushed to meet the retreating armies to learn firsthand about the conditions among the soldiers, and some, encountering Izu among them, would linger and chat with him. Private Petrică Buciuc's suspicions about Izu's actions were rising like dough:

"Who are those guys always talking to the Jew?" he asked

his comrades curiously.

The men shrugged indifferently and went about their business. After one encounter with a well-known reporter, Petrică boldly confronted Izu:

"Iţic, who was that guy you were talking to?"

"An old colleague."

"What's he doing here?"

"I don't know! He works for a newspaper."

"And what did you tell him?"

"That's none of your business, what I told him"

"Iţic, see this razor?" Petrică said, pulling a pocketknife from his coat. "This is what I'll 'settle' you with if you betray us! Got that? With this!"

"Are you out of your mind? Why are you threatening me?"

"Because you people are born traitors..."

Izu felt the blood rush to his head, but his voice, strangled by the cruelty of the insult, caught in his throat. He found nothing better to do than turn his back on Petrică in disgust. Just then, Tudor was returning from the latrines. His face, yellowed like wax, was sunken now, and he felt a fever coming on. Izu moved to greet him, but Petrică stepped in his way:

"You think he can protect you? Remember this: the razor!"

It didn't take long for Sergeant Salciu to hear that Izu had been speaking with the reporters. The next morning, during roll call, he pulled him in front of the platoon:

"Is it true you talked to the journalists who came here?"

"Yes, sir!"

"And what connection do you have with them?"

"I used to work at a newspaper. That's how they know me."

"Which newspaper?"

"Adevărul."

"What did you do there?"

"Reports."

"Then what are you doing here?"

"I'm doing my duty!"

"What duty, man? Who needs your duty? I think you came here to spy on us! What do you say to that? Isn't it true?"

"It's not true, Sergeant! I don't need them to write—I can do that on my own!... I haven't done it so far, but if you push me, I could write about how you're insulting me in front of my comrades."

"What was that? I'm insulting you. I'll show you an insult

now! Soldier Buciuc!"

"Yes, sir!"

"Take this one with you! From now on, you're responsible for him! Wherever he goes, you go too! Understood?"

"Understood, sir!"

"If he talks to a civilian again, you be there—and report it to me! Back in formation!"

As he fell back into the ranks, Petrică Buciuc hissed through his teeth at Izu:

"What the hell am I supposed to do with you; you damn nuisance? What do you mean, *I'm* responsible for you?"

"Isn't that what you wanted? Didn't you rat me out for talking to that guy?"

"Well, wasn't it true?"

Izu said nothing. For the first time, he found himself surrounded by the hatred of people he had done no harm to. Even back home, in the neighborhood where he had grown up and gone to school all his life, he had known the oppressive weight of antisemitism. He had always been called *jidán*—a slur for Jew—and the name Iţic followed him wherever he went. Small obstacles had always been thrown in his path, yet people were more understanding there. He had even found sympathy, sometimes admiration, just like

Tudor had, who had become a true friend among those people. But never had he encountered such bitter hatred and open hostility as now. He had known Petrică Buciuc despised him from the start. But now, under Buciuc's watch, he could no longer speak to anyone—possibly not even to Tudor—and there was nothing he could do to change the situation.

He had volunteered, willingly, to serve under arms, with the noblest intentions, just as his father had done during the War of Independence. But the inherited prejudices of ordinary men turned all that was good into hatred and revenge. There weren't many like that, but they were hard to stand up against. At the same time, he didn't know whether he would still be allowed to stay close to Tudor, with whom he had formed a sincere and lasting friendship. Was that friendship now also about to fall apart?

Izu remembered all the articles he had read about the "Dreyfus Affair." The whole story had made waves in France just a few years ago and had spread like wildfire around the world. It was about the Jewish captain Alfred Dreyfus in the French army, wrongfully accused by his superiors of espionage and passing secret documents to the Germans during the war over Alsace. In 1894, he was sentenced to life of hard labor and sent to serve his time on Devil's Island, the most dreaded prison in the South Atlantic, near French Guiana. Convinced of his innocence, his brother Mathieu Dreyfus reopened the case, exposing the flimsiness of the accusations and revealing that it was not Dreyfus, but Count Ferdinand Walsin Esterházy, a major on the General Staff, who had passed secret documents to the Germans—the true traitor. Yet the case was closed again, with an even harsher sentence for Dreyfus.

Only because of public opinion, especially the open letter *"J'accuse!"* by Emile Zola, addressed to the President of France and published in the newspaper *L'Aurore* on January 13, 1898—stirring a massive public reaction—was the case finally reviewed by the Court of Cassation in 1906. Alfred Dreyfus was freed, returned to France, and reinstated with all his rights. The Dreyfus Affair had shown the world the horrific consequences of unjustified antisemitic policies used by extremist parties to maintain their grip on power.

Tudor, who usually impressed everyone with his cheerful and self-possessed nature, had now lost his characteristic vitality. It started after he ate some unripe fruit and drank water afterward. At first, he didn't pay much attention to the stomach cramps, but when he noticed he had developed terrible diarrhea, he treated himself with Epsom salts to clear it out. That completely flushed his intestines, and he thought he had recovered—but he hadn't. He managed for another day or two, until a fever set in, accompanied by vomiting. Izu reported his condition to the nurse from the ambulance unit, and she decided to send him to a Red Cross hospital.

"I have to go with him!" Izu insisted. "We've been together

this whole time! If he's sick, there's no way I'm not."

"But you have no fever," the nurse said, after checking his pulse and feeling the skin around his neck.

"That's impossible! We've been like brothers. We were always together, we slept next to each other, ate the same food, drank the same water. If I haven't gotten sick yet, I've caught it from him, and it's just a matter of time."

"Possible. Go with him!"

The Hell

The barrack was drowned in darkness, pierced only by the faint glow of a few oil lamps hanging here and there from the wooden ceiling of the ward. A few more lanterns were mounted on the walls. Monsignor Vladimir Ghica, dressed in a white coat over the black clothes he wore underneath, was keeping vigil beside the bed of a patient admitted that day. The man lay sprawled across the bed, muttering incoherent words in delirium and tossing restlessly, as if struggling against someone. At that late hour of the day, the monsignor was surprised to see Princess Maria step into the ward, accompanied by Dr. Cădere and Mura, the young woman who often accompanied the princess. The new arrivals seemed anxious to assess the condition of the patient. The monsignor stepped aside, greeting them with a quiet nod.

"Is he conscious?" Maria asked.

"He's delirious."

"What is he saying?"

"I can't make much sense of it. Sometimes he talks to someone, but I can't understand what he says. Other times, he seems to speak to someone he calls *father*, saying something about flowers at the cemetery and other such things..."

"Is it serious? Does he have a chance?" Maria now asked Dr. Cădere.

"Let's see how he responds to the medication. He needs intravenous rehydration—he's lost a lot of fluids. He's very weak, but I believe he'll recover."

Maria exhaled in relief. From behind her, Mura gazed at Tudor, visibly moved. He was almost unrecognizable, with a sunburnt face, unshaven for days, and eyelids fluttering restlessly as if searching for someone behind them. His breathing was labored, causing the medal with the Virgin Mary—gifted to him by Maria— to rise and fall erratically on his chest. In her eyes welled up a boundless compassion for the man she had seen at the start of the summer, so full of health, confidence, and joy for life. Now, tossing on the bed of suffering in this infernal ward, where death seemed to reign, she wondered whether Monsignor Ghica, missionary and holy man, had prayed for this poor soul as well.

Maria took a longer look around her. The crimson-colored walls of the barrack, the dimness of the room, the suffocating heat inside, and the lingering smell of vomit were hard to bear. Monsignor Ghica and another nurse moved from one patient to another, monitoring each one's condition, administering medication, changing lines, and cleaning up the vomit that came frequently in the advanced stage of the illness. She could not hide her admiration for these people—true angels—who, through their dedication, fought to save the lives of others, neglecting their own. Some would be saved, others would succumb to the disease, but in the days to come, new patients would take their place. And so, the struggle would go on, unceasingly, until the epidemic was finally eradicated. Never had she witnessed such bravery. Before leaving, Maria went over to shake the hands of the monsignor and the nurse.

"Do you know this patient?" the monsignor asked.

"Yes. I met him in Comănești. He's a teacher there. Before enlisting, he came to say goodbye to me."

"I see. May the Lord help him."

"May the Lord help us all."

"There's another soldier who came with him," the monsignor added. "He said they're friends. He insisted I let him stay by his side and take care of him, but I didn't allow it. He's waiting around the barracks, hoping for news of his friend."

Maria looked closely at the monsignor's face.

"How did he end up here?"

"He came with the ambulance. He said that if his comrade is sick, then he can't possibly be healthy."

"Has he been examined by a doctor?"

"I have no idea..."

"Mura, please. There's a soldier outside waiting for news about Tudor. Tell him not to leave until he's spoken to me!"

"Yes, ma'am."

As she stepped outside, Mura found the soldier sitting on the step at the entrance of the barrack. At the sound of the door opening, Izu stood up, thinking the monsignor was bringing news about Tudor. But instead, a slender figure dressed entirely in white like a nurse appeared—and as soon as she saw him, she approached:

"Are you Mr. Tudor's friend?"

"Yes, ma'am! How is he?" asked Izu.

"For now, he's lying down, but he's under a doctor's care. Her Highness, Princess Maria, wishes to speak with you. Please don't leave."

"The Princess?" Izu asked, stunned.

Maria, also dressed in a long white robe, her hair covered with a matching scarf, came out of the barracks, accompanied by Dr. Cădere, and walked toward Izu.

"You're the one who brought Tudor?" the princess asked.

"Yes, Your Highness!"

"He's under Dr. Cădere's care, but you're not allowed to stay here! Were you and Tudor vaccinated?"

"No, Your Highness..."

"Go with Dr. Cădere now—he'll examine you, and then you'll be placed in a vaccination and prevention center."

"Yes, but what about Tudor?"

"Dr. Cădere and Mura will keep you updated about him."

King Carol had come in person to see what was happening on the Romanian banks of the Danube, where all troops had to be evacuated from Bulgaria by that Thursday, August 28, 1913. Until then, some troops had been held on the opposite bank for triage—sorting the sick or feverish from the healthy. Now, however, the last columns were crossing the river either on bridges set up by engineers or transported by boats toward garrisons in the east of the country, through Galați and Brăila.

The overcrowding of people, supplies, and animals, the disorder among troops, the often-contradictory orders, and the frustration of the soldiers—who, though back on Romanian soil, were forced to wait in quarantine when they were so close to home—all hindered the smooth operations of those responsible for handling the situation.

At one point in the Danube lazarettos, especially in Zimnicea, bread couldn't be provided for all the soldiers due to the sudden influx of the sick and suspected cases. Even hot food became an issue for the same reasons.

During the two days of the King's inspection, he saw the situation with his own eyes, received reports from commanders, doctors, nurses, and even soldiers under observation, who voiced their justified desire to go home—autumn was coming, and the fields had not yet been sown.

These days, during her spare moments, Maria finds time to visit the sick, handing out flowers, cigarettes, chocolate, and other treats, always checking in on their condition. In the dreadful place known as "Hell," Tudor Avădanei—under the daily care of Dr. Cădere and nightly watch of Monsignor Ghica—gradually began to recover. The downward spiral was halted, and hope for his recovery significantly increased. Once the fever and delirium subsided, during Maria's morning visit, Tudor managed to sit up against the iron headboard of the bed. Recognizing the smiling face of the princess behind the white nurse's robe, he tried to say her name, surprised:

"Maria?"

"Yes, Mr. Tudor, it's me! I'm so glad you're better today!"

"Domniță, I didn't think I'd survive this illness, but I never imagined I'd see you here, among the sick. I don't even know how I got here, I can't remember who brought me."

"A friend brought you. A comrade, Mr. Haimovici."

"Izu? He's here too?"

"He is. Don't worry now, your fever's rising again. He hasn't fallen ill; he's in quarantine. You'll see each other once you're well," Maria said, helping him lie back down.

Behind the princess, Mura stood smiling, holding an armful of flowers. It seemed Tudor didn't remember, but she had spent many hours in recent days by his side, comforting him with a gentle touch, wiping the sweat from his fevered brow, or helping him sip water when he asked.

Maria took a red rose from Mura's bundle and placed it on the pillow beside Tudor. He let himself be cared for like a child, moved, even joyful—as if the whole moment were part of a dream.

Expropriation, a New Idea

In Bucharest, there was great agitation at the time. The Conservatives, led by Titu Maiorescu, had lost the cohesion they had shown during the peace negotiations. Now, Maiorescu and Marghiloman, dissatisfied with Take Ionescu's scheming during the peace conference, were threatening to split the party. On the other side, Take Ionescu, offended by criticism from his fellow ministers as well as from opposition liberals, tried to defend himself, and the resulting tensions caused a stagnation in addressing major issues, which continued to be delayed.

Since the peasant uprising of 1907, none of the government's promises to improve the agrarian situation had materialized. Many young progressives—even those associated with the *Junimea* society led by Titu Maiorescu—began distancing themselves, leaning instead toward the National Liberal Party, led by Ion I. C. Brătianu, who emphasized the urgency of enacting reforms.

After returning from the Second Balkan War, Ionel Brătianu was guided by two priorities that could no longer be postponed. First, the army needed to be strengthened and equipped with everything it required. Second, the long-discussed but unimplemented reforms had to be carried out as soon as possible. Foremost among these reforms was the revision of the Constitution, which would enable the abolition of the existing electoral colleges and, at the same time, allow for agrarian reform.

In Brătianu's vision, agrarian reform could only be achieved through the expropriation of the large estates owned by Romania's political-agrarian oligarchy. In early September 1913, Ionel Brătianu published an open letter in *Viitorul*, the central publication of the National Liberal Party, addressed to His Majesty King Carol I, in which he laid out the need to allocate 2.2 million hectares of expropriated land to peasants. These lands were held by the great landlords of the national oligarchy.

At that time, no one—absolutely no one—anywhere in the world had dared to think or even utter the word "expropriation," yet the concept would later become standard policy across the rest of Europe, with the notable exception of Russia. That country would soon pay dearly for ignoring its significance, a mistake that helped trigger the great revolution of 1917.

Ionel Brătianu's letter created an enormous stir across the country. It generated both interest and enthusiasm on one side, and harsh criticism, accusations, and polemics on the other. Nicolae Filipescu, writing in the newspaper *Epoca*, put forth the theory that the liberals' promises were not sincere. Meanwhile, Maiorescu and Marghiloman claimed that the liberals were preparing to implement revolutionary, anarchist measures. Nevertheless, in the wake of that letter, the days of Titu Maiorescu's government began to appear numbered. Even the king himself foresaw the need to change the government by the end of the year.

At Brătianu's request, the king granted him an audience at Peleş Castle. But before traveling there, Brătianu convened the leading members of the National Liberal Party at his residence on Lascăr Catargiu Street, where he laid out his plan in detail. What stood out most to those present was the enthusiasm with which Brătianu's ideas were received—not only by the younger members who formed the party's left wing, but even by the veterans who had once collaborated with his father, I.C. Brătianu. Even those who owned large estates—whose lands would be subject to expropriation—approved the plan unanimously, once Brătianu made his position clear from the outset:

"If you do not share my way of seeing things, gentlemen, then I ask you to choose another leader!"[xxxiv]

For two days, the Liberal Party members made a point of reassuring Brătianu that his plan had their full support and that they urged him to remain at the helm of the party and carry out the proposed reforms. Confident in his party's unity, Brătianu presented his views on the internal situation to King Carol during their audience. He stated plainly that he could not accept the post of future prime minister unless he was permitted to carry out these two major reforms.

King Carol—by nature resistant to reforms after 47 years of a reign marked by enormous achievements in nearly every field—nevertheless agreed to allow the reforms to go forward. He placed one condition, however: they had to be introduced with moderation, the overly democratic zeal of the younger members needed to be tempered, and the reforms had to be incorporated into the Constitution in cooperation with the opposition party.

During this time, the National Liberal Party began preparing the public for the introduction of the new reforms through a series of conferences across the country, with speakers well-prepared to answer all questions and explain why these reforms were necessary. The first of these conferences took place in Bucharest, in the "Liedertafel" hall, with Ionel Brătianu as speaker. After him, the majority landowners, the right wing of the party, chose to read personal statements in favor of expropriation, so as not to be forced to answer questions.

During the frequent meetings between King Carol and Brătianu, the sovereign informed the future prime minister that Titu Maiorescu had signed the renewal of the alliance treaty with the Central Powers (the Triple Alliance), originally concluded in 1883 and kept secret from public opinion over the years, even after its extension in 1902 and again the previous year.

If in 1883 adherence to this treaty had been a necessary act for the development of the young independent Romanian state, seeking a period of peace to consolidate its position through the guarantee of the great powers that would intervene in the event of external attacks, now the situation was entirely different. First of all, the Central Powers had weakened; Otto von Bismarck, the great statesman who had steered the fate of Europe in the second half of the 19th century, had died in 1898, leaving behind a desolate world. Now the Alliance needed Romania more than Romania needed the Alliance, considering that the Austro-Hungarian heir, Archduke Franz Ferdinand, supported the Romanians of Transylvania in their struggle against forced denationalization imposed by Hungary. Even Count Tisza recognized that the situation could not continue as it was. Upon hearing this news, Brătianu was struck with consternation:

"Titu Maiorescu signed this act without a single condition. No attempt to change anything, to improve the situation of those in Transylvania, who were not mentioned at all in the new treaty. Although Maiorescu himself was from Transylvania, he showed a servility that is unforgivable."

At the same time, Brătianu began to realize that the king, visibly aged in recent times, no longer had the critical vision of the past and, guided by advisors like Maiorescu and Petre Carp—who would say: *"In foreign policy, I look to what Vienna and Berlin say;*

that's where the center of gravity of our foreign policy lies, not in Bucharest"—had let slip the possibility of securing advantages in signing this treaty.

"Your Majesty, in case of war, I and the National Liberal Party cannot respect this treaty!" said Brătianu after reading the document, which only the king, the prime minister, and the foreign minister knew about.

"Why?" asked the king, who was ill that day, not only physically, as his health was deteriorating by the day, but also morally, seeing that his subjects were beginning to oppose his decisions.

"I don't believe you'll find a government capable of applying the conditions of a renewed alliance under these circumstances,"[xxxv] Brătianu replied. "I believe that Germany, which more than once had to intervene objectively in the relations between the Austro-Hungarian monarchy and its subjects in Transylvania, had a moral duty to prevent future problems before signing the treaty, which Mr. Maiorescu so easily signed."

The king remained silent and troubled after the discussion with his future prime minister—a discussion that only deepened his prior state of depression. Brătianu would later repeat the same accusations to the German chargé d'affaires in Bucharest, Count Waldburg.

Convalescence

Before finishing his shift of the previous night, though tired and deeply saddened by the death of six patients, Monsignor Vladimir Ghica stopped by Tudor's bed. Tudor was awake and showing signs of shaking off the illness.

"How are you, my son? How are you feeling?"

"Good morning, Father! I'm feeling better, thank you! I think I can get up now and return to my unit, to my comrades…"

"Not yet, my son! You're not fully recovered, and you might still spread the illness to others. Maybe in a day or two, you'll be able to move to the convalescent barracks, until you're completely well."

Tudor looked at the man sitting on the edge of his bed. He had an oval face, with a wide forehead, mustache and goatee, white hair cut short, and lively eyes that radiated calm and kindness. He knew, like everyone else, that this man came from a distinguished line of country rulers and held a princely title, but his demeanor was simple and kind, like that of any ordinary man. He liked to talk with the sick and encourage them.

"Father, people call you Monsignor. Are you a priest?"

"No, my son! I'm a layman. I studied in France. There are

no Orthodox churches there, so I attended a Protestant church. That drew me more toward the Catholic faith, but I can't practice it because my mother is deeply devoted to the Orthodox faith, and I don't want to upset her at her age. So, I decided to carry out the Lord's work as a layman."

"I think you're a saint!" said Tudor, moved by Monsignor Ghica's words.

"Saints are in heaven, my son. I'm just a man trying to do a little good," answered the Monsignor as he rose to leave. "God be with you!"

After Dr. Cădere's morning visit, Mura came by to check on Tudor:

"Good morning! Her Highness sent me to see how you are. Are you feeling better?"

"Much better. Please thank Her Highness on my behalf. Would you stay and talk with me for a bit, if you can? Mura, that's your name, isn't it?"

"Yes, Mura is my name."

"What a beautiful name! Mura sounds like—how to say it— like a poem. Like a sunlit grove. I think that during my illness, you appeared to me like the sun itself. I don't know if it was a dream or real. You're always close to your lady, you seem like sisters…"

"Her Highness is so good to me!... I try to help her," the girl replied shyly.

"I understand. Have you seen my friend who brought me here?"

"Mr. Haimovici? He always asks how you're doing. I think I'll go tell him I've seen you."

"Please, call me Tudor, by my first name, without "mister." And tell Izu I thank him, that I owe him my life." Tudor took the girl's hand, looking intently into her eyes:

"You'll come back to see me, won't you?"

The girl smiled, blushing as she gently pulled her hand away from his:

"I'll come back!"

After she left, Tudor looked across the long hall lined with beds along the walls, with groaning patients in them. The Sisters of Charity tending to them were administering medicine and food, the orderlies were changing bedding or cleaning, and the doctor was giving brief orders. Those who had died during the night were carried out on stretchers through a side door. Tudor wondered where they were taking their bodies—back home, or would they be buried there.? Besides the monsignor, were there other priests present to say a Christian prayer over their burial? He wanted to ask someone, but no one had the time to answer his questions.

During his inspection of the hospitals along the Danube, King Carol grasped the seriousness of the issues that had arisen once all the troops returning from Bulgaria were concentrated in that area. Many soldiers were gravely ill, and others were suffering in varying degrees from the cholera epidemic, which under no circumstances could anyone be allowed to spread further into the country. They needed to be quartered, fed, and kept in quarantine for ten days before being sent back to their units. But how could he manage an army numbering no fewer than four hundred thousand soldiers, with limited medical personnel, insufficient medicine, and so many soldiers eager to return to their homes?

Many of the specialists he spoke with, like the Doctor Captain Slătineanu, who oversaw the screening of troops stationed at Zimnicea–Târgu Măgurele, or Doctor Mezinceanu, who believed it would be far more effective to allow the troops to return to their local units, where health and hygiene could be managed more easily. As a result, a number of units that had been vaccinated with at least one dose, after the isolation of the sick or suspected cholera cases, were loaded onto trains and sent to their garrisons. But this only partially eased the burden on the doctors, who struggled from dawn till dusk to meet all demands, to pay attention to each patient, and to heal as many as possible—if only the body, not the soul—of those fighting to survive the illness. The sisters and all the medical staff were subjected to the same superhuman effort, battling exhaustion, standing on their feet for long hours, enduring the conditions imposed by basic shortages affecting food, hygiene, and rest—all of which were largely ignored.

Princess Marie was no exception. On August 30, 1913, she wrote in her personal diary: *"For a week now I've been living in the midst of cholera—organizing, improvising, keeping things together. I didn't think I'd be capable of this, or that I could bear such a thing, but the immense difficulties and the constant need to give courage to others keep me fighting. I'm at the center of an enormous lazaretto for cholera patients who depend entirely on me. I've changed—I'm almost a different person. I live here nearly full-time, all orders are given by me, all supplies, medicines, blankets are distributed by me."*[xxxvi]

Apart from everything else, it was her constant daily presence in every corner of the Zimnicea lazaretto that served as the true balm for the sick. They saw in her a white angel, with radiant, serene eyes and an ever-present smile—just like the flowers she laid each day on the pillows of patients too weak to receive them from her delicate hand, tirelessly working to soothe their suffering. There was not a soul who did not bless this cherished and awaited presence, the most precious remedy that gave them strength to overcome the illness and all its hardships.

In one of those corners of the lazaretto lay Petrică Buciuc, suspected of infection and held back at the triage station while the rest of his company had already been dispatched to their base garrison. The Princess's unpretentious visit surprised him especially when she stopped at his bedside to ask his name, where he was from, and what was ailing him. Accompanied by the on-duty doctor and Mura, her arms full of flowers, Maria's questions didn't feel at all like the formalities of someone fulfilling a duty, but came from genuine concern, especially since she immediately asked the doctor to confirm his medical condition. From that moment, the image of that white-clad figure would become the object of his constant gaze, following her everywhere in the ward and beyond, as if drawn by some magnetic force that would not let him tear his eyes away from her.

Then something entirely unexpected caught his attention. Outside the barracks, just after Maria had exited his ward, Petrică Buciuc couldn't believe his eyes when he saw Izu—the same man who had slipped through his finger's days earlier in Bulgaria—alive and unharmed, now standing right in front of Princess Maria, engaged in a lively conversation.

Watching them from afar through the ward's grimy window, Petrică couldn't make out what they were saying, but what puzzled him wasn't Izu's presence—it was that the illustrious Princess was speaking to him, gesturing broadly and taking her time to explain something he couldn't decipher.

"Did the Princess know that guy's a Jew? Petrică wondered. Not just a Jew—he might be a spy too."

Petrică's soul was gnawed from within, as though mole-like claws were digging fresh tunnels through the coal of hatred he held for the wicked Jew who kept appearing in his path. He instinctively felt the smooth surface of his pocketknife, remembering how he had once warned Izu what might happen if he didn't back off. But clearly, the man hadn't understood.

It wouldn't take much for fate to catch up with him here.

Out of Affection

During the morning rounds, Doctor Cădere informed Tudor that later in the day an orderly would transfer him to the ward for patients who had recovered from the illness but were still under observation. Not long after, Mura came to check on how he was feeling. Tudor shared with her what the doctor had said.

"I'm glad. That means you'll probably be able to go home very soon," the girl remarked.

"I think so too," Tudor replied, "but I'll miss seeing you and Domnița every day like I do here."

"I think we'll come back to the villa in Copăceni," Mura reassured him. "Then you can see us again."

"Mura, do you mind if I ask you something?"

"What is it?"

"Well, it's not easy for me to say this," Tudor said, blushing. "But I'd be happy if you came with me there, to Copăceni... Would you want to?"

The girl looked at him, caught off guard. No one had ever asked her a question like that before. In her twenty-two years, always in the company of the Princess, she had seen much, heard much, and understood much—but no one had ever dared to propose to her or ask for her hand in life. And now she herself had started to wonder what kind of future awaited her. Would she remain an old maid, a spinster all her life, serving in the shadow of the future queen? Because her service had no set schedule for day or night, and the kind of family she dreamed of, with children raised and educated in her spirit, seemed impossible under such conditions.

On the other hand, Tudor wanted to take her there, to Copăceni, to his home and village where he had spent his whole life. But she had always lived in castles and palaces, with many servants preparing everything for her and Her Highness. How would she manage in a simple house she'd never seen, where she would have to take care of everything herself? How would she get along with the people around them?

Tudor was thirteen years older than her. He was a good man, serious, and it was clear he cared about her, even though they had only recently met. She knew these things from her lady, who had told her that he'd been a widower for eight years and still mourned his late wife. She liked Tudor too—probably more than she could fully understand—but now, caught by surprise at his sudden question, she didn't know what to say:

"I don't know! Her Highness needs me. I can't just leave her, suddenly. Why do you want me to come with you?"

"Because, because..." Tudor stammered, trying to sit up by holding onto the edge of the bed. He wanted to say something tender, but at the same time he felt a lump in his throat that made it hard to speak.

"You see, Mura? You've been so kind to me! You've become dear to me... Very dear!"

The girl remained silent. The two of them stayed there, gazing deeply into each other's eyes, studying one another's faces like children who didn't know what to do. After a moment, flustered, Tudor tried to take her hand in his, and she let it rest lightly, carried by his palm, seared by the touch.

"Do you feel something for me too?" Tudor asked.

Mura lowered her gaze, nodding slightly as her cheeks flushed with heat.

"Mura, my dear! You have no idea how happy you've made me! I feel like flying, bed and all, with you in it! You're the one I've been waiting for, year after year until now! I searched for you, I waited for you, and when I thought you'd never appear, the miracle became true—you're here, like an angel in this den of death. You'll never know how much I've missed you! Shall I tell Domniţa when she comes today that I want you to be my wife?"

"Not yet! Let me tell her first—prepare her a little..." the girl said as she stood up to leave.

Tudor was still holding her hand, but releasing it, he wrapped his blanket around his body and tried to stand up. Mura gently stopped him, pressing lightly on his shoulders.

"Don't get up! I'll come see you later!"

Tudor watched her graceful figure weave through the rows of beds toward the door. Luck, a miracle, an unimaginable joy—after that terrible illness he had barely survived—had filled him with a surge of energy he had never felt before. Everything seemed unreal.

He couldn't grasp how it had happened, how such a gentle creature, beautiful like a fairy and pure as an angel, had come into his life and offered herself to him—a simple man from the countryside, a widower who had suffered so much.

Overwhelmed by happiness, he didn't know what to do with himself. He sat there in silence, contemplating the ward of suffering around him, feeling as though he were suffocating among the dying. He could no longer wait passively to be allowed outside, into the fresh air and freedom, to give full rein to the storm of emotion exploding within him.

It wasn't long before an orderly came in with clean clothes, telling him to change, he was to be moved to the observation ward for those who had passed the critical stage. After receiving his second vaccination, he would be sent back to his unit in the country. Upon hearing the orderly's words, Tudor stood up and, making the sign of the cross, whispered just loud enough for himself to hear:

"God help me!"

Izu

Izu was eager to see Princess Maria one more time, because that morning Dr. Cădere had informed him that he was cleared to return to his unit—he had to leave. He insisted on being allowed to visit Tudor before leaving the camp, but the doctor told him it was beyond his authority, so he couldn't help. His only hope lay in the princess's influence, she had always been so understanding. But she was like quicksilver, never staying in one place, and in such a vast camp as this one, with dozens of barracks, tents, and thousands of soldiers crammed into them, it was difficult to know where she might be found—or if she even had time to speak with him.

That's why Izu decided to wait in the open area at the center of the camp, where the country's flag fluttered atop a tall pole. Even just crossing the camp from one end to the other took considerable effort—not to mention the heat or the frequent late-summer downpours. Yet the princess, always accompanied by a few aides, made this effort daily, and more than once a day. Izu marveled at how she managed to do it with such energy. At the same time, without showing any signs of fatigue, she spoke with every patient, brought them supplies, accepted their letters to mail, rewarded them with flowers and that unique smile that never left her face when she spoke to someone.

From everything he'd heard, every soldier—whether hospitalized or on duty—every doctor, nurse, or orderly, regardless of rank or social status, was captivated by the personality, devotion, and beauty of this young woman. She had managed to jolt the entire camp's operation out of inertia through her exemplary conduct and tireless spirit of sacrifice, something no one else could match.

Seated on the step of one of the barracks, Izu waited for her to appear, leisurely inhaling the smoke from a cigarette from the pack he'd received the previous day from the princess. Instead of her, he saw Mura coming out of the "Hell" ward and went to meet her.

"Good morning. Have you seen Tudor?"

"Yes! He's doing well. Today he's being discharged from that ward, but he'll stay a few more days in the camp, under observation."

"I was told I'm free to leave, but I want to see Tudor before I go," Izu informed her.

"Probably today, after he's released from here," the girl replied.

"Probably. I'd like to thank Her Highness—and you—for all the kindness you've shown me. Do you think I could see the princess?"

"I suppose so. If you can't, I'll tell her myself!" Mura assured him.

"Thanks! I'll wait here for Tudor. You're a remarkable person—I'm grateful to you!"

"Mr. Haimovici, you've done far more for Tudor. He says you saved his life. You're a true friend!"

After parting from Mura, Izu resumed his place on the step. Activity in the space between the barracks was limited, since no one was allowed to move from one barrack to another, except for doctors and certain medical staff. Even those under observation were forbidden from leaving the designated perimeter of their barrack, except when necessary to use the latrines, which had been installed at a certain distance from the rest of the facilities.

After enough time had passed for Izu to smoke another cigarette or two, Tudor emerged from "Hell" accompanied by an orderly. He looked drawn and much thinner than Izu was used to seeing him. He wore a clean but slightly crumpled uniform, freshly disinfected, and he squinted as if blinded by the bright sunlight. Izu rose from the step that had kept him company and joyfully stepped forward to greet his friend.

"Tudor! Thank God! You made it!"

Tudor, startled as if awakened from a dream, only then

spotted his friend and overjoyed, opened his arms to embrace him.

"Brother, Izu! I'm so glad to see you! Hold still, let me look at you for a second! You're just the same as I remember. What would I have done without you? I wouldn't have made it this far! Were you sick too?"

"No. I didn't catch anything, but I was afraid I would. Now they've put me on the list to return to the regiment."

"When?"

"Now! Soon, today..."

"And when will I see you again?"

"Ask for me at the newspaper. Leave word and I'll come find you," Izu replied.

Just then, a shadow flashed like lightning behind Izu and Tudor's escort, and a blade gleamed in the sunlight as it plunged into the soldier's side, catching him completely off guard. Tudor froze in horror as he saw his friend collapse to the ground. Only then did he catch sight of Petrică Buciuc's triumphant expression as he shouted:

"I warned him! I told him, but he wouldn't listen! He asked for it, he—"

Tudor hurled himself at the attacker, wrapping his arms around Petrică's shoulders and trying to strangle him from behind.

But Petrică, stronger than he was, bent forward, twisted around, and lashed out blindly with the knife, stabbing backward into Tudor's bony thighs as he tried to tighten his grip around the man's neck. Only when the orderly intervened did they manage to subdue Petrică, and with the help of several other soldiers who had appeared seemingly out of nowhere, they tied the attacker's hands behind his back. He kept screaming, ignored by everyone:

"He's a kike! Don't you get it? A Jew! He had to be wiped out!"

Tudor bent over the body of his friend, who had fallen face-down on the bare earth, now stained red by the blood spilling from the open wound in Izu's chest. He tried to turn him over, but alone, he could manage no more than to glimpse his face, those terrified eyes and a mouth that seemed to try and speak, though only a gurgling breath, flooded with blood, came out. Izu died in his friend's arms.

Tudor felt his heart tear apart in anguish and could not hold back the pitiful, unmanly tears that flooded his face, even as the orderly and another soldier tried to help him to his feet. He could stand only on one leg; the other had been slashed in several places by Petrică Buciuc's blade. His trousers, gaiters, and boots were soaked and sticky with the clotted blood from his wounds. Not far from his feet, half-buried in the dust, lay the knife that had caused it all.

Among the crowd of onlookers that had gathered, Princess Maria and Mura appeared. The sight was ghastly: Izu sprawled in a pool of blood, Tudor held upright by two soldiers, his face streaked with tears, the bundle of clean laundry that had been meant for him scattered on the ground, and the bloodied knife—its blade still open—lying as silent witness to the horror that had just occurred. With one glance, Maria understood everything except the motive behind the massacre. She asked Tudor:

"What happened?"

"A former comrade from our company, Petrică Buciuc, held a grudge against Izu for being Jewish. When he saw him here, talking to me, he came at him from behind with a knife and killed him."

"Where is the killer?"

"They took him somewhere—I don't know..."

"You fought him? You're hurt, I can see that."

Tudor nodded faintly. Mura, her eyes brimming with tears, stepped in to support Tudor by the arm, seeing how he could barely stand. Maria ordered that two stretchers be bought, one for Izu, the other for Tudor. Izu was taken to the tent where the dead awaited burial. The wounds on Tudor's thigh were deep but not life-threatening. Mura stayed by his side until he was bandaged and transferred to a ward for wounded soldiers.

"I don't know where he came from. I didn't see him until it was to late. I can't explain it... he appeared like a ghost!" Tudor said, trying to recall the moment just before the attack.

There was so much sorrow in his eyes that it brought Mura to tears as well. Both had just spoken with Izu not long before, and now both held in their minds the image of that young man with a simple face, intelligent black eyes that lit up his expression with trust and warmth—a face marked by a slightly hooked nose and a modest, gentle smile. He had stood apart from most of his fellow soldiers through his shyness, his restraint from ever offending anyone—even when insulted for his ethnicity—and especially through his wise, measured view of everything happening around him. He preferred to not involve himself in disputes that didn't concern him directly, and when he had to intervene, he did so with the same calm, reasoned clarity, free of bias or anger—an approach others could not find fault. But now, the flame of his quiet light had been extinguished forever, leaving only its warm glow in the hearts of those who had admired him—now overcome by the weight of bitter regret.

After leaving the scene of the incident, Princess Maria went to speak with Lieutenant Colonel Nicolae Rujinschi, commander of the Zimnicea camp, asking him to send Petrică Buciuc before the Military Tribunal to stand trial for premeditated murder. The commander assured her that the accused was in custody and would be sent to Bucharest to face trial.

Maria then consulted Monsignor Vladimir Ghica. There was no rabbi present in the camp to perform the burial according to the Mosaic rites in which Izu had been born. But she knew that the monsignor had traveled the world in his humanitarian missions, including to Palestine, had studied the Scriptures in their original languages, and was the most knowledgeable person available regarding Jewish burial customs.

Both the monsignor and the princess had known Izu and shared the same sorrow over the tragic death of this young man who had left them with the impression of a noble character. They agreed that the following morning, after the burial service for the other soldiers deceased in the camp, Izu would be laid to rest in the presence of those who had known him—not with pomp, but in accordance with the rites of his faith.

Mura

All that remained for Maria to do now was to see what would become of Tudor, this man hounded by a fate resembling that of Job from bible. Like him, Tudor had lost everything dearest to him: his wife, his child, and now his friend. Time and again, despite the sincere and exemplary devotion he had shown, Tudor remained isolated in his own solitude, as if cursed. On her way to the barracks where she knew she'd find him; Maria couldn't shake her sorrow for this man who deserved more joy from life.

She found him lying on a cot, with a pair of crutches propped beside it. Mura was sitting on the edge of the bed, contemplating his pain-stricken face. When Tudor saw the princess, he tried to lift himself up on his elbows. His right thigh was wrapped in white bandages all the way up to where the femur meets the pelvis. His arm—still bruised from the chokehold he had used on Petrică Buciuc—was also bandaged to cover knife wounds from the attacker. Maria looked at him in silence, unsure of what to say.

Mura stood up at the princess's arrival and, wringing her hands, said:

"Ma'am, Mr. Tudor asked me if I would be his wife..."

"And what did you say?" Maria asked after a moment of

silence.

"That I needed to speak with Your Highness first."

Maria rested her hands on the footboard of Tudor's bed, surprised by the sudden turn of events. What could she say? Tudor was a good man; one she had long wished she could help in some way—bring a little light into his life. But Mura? Was Mura the right person for him? No, that couldn't be. Her dear Mura could shine like Cinderella in a prince's palace—or in the life of any man who sought a wife with her intelligence and education, her beauty, modesty, and most notable, her deep loyalty.

Maria had always regarded Mura as a trusted friend, almost like a sister. She was the one person in whom she could confide even when surrounded by enemies and spies in her own home. Mura had known her suffering and brought her comfort.

When Maria first came to the country, Mura had been no more than two years old. Maria first met her in the household of Nando's servants, and that sweet child had grown into a living doll. Maria used to wish her own unborn child—Carol—might look just like her. Later, when Carol and Elisabeta were being tutored, Mura, their playmate, joined them in their lessons. Slightly older and more disciplined than her own children, Mura quickly mastered foreign languages, and all the learning expected of a cultured young woman. Her presence alongside Maria during trips abroad had refined in her the grace of a true lady of society—someone Maria had often proudly introduced as her "little friend". And now, Tudor wanted to take her away? By what right?

Maria thought hard. She needed to help them both see for themselves that they were not meant for each other. She had to explain the gap between them in such a way that they would conclude—on their own—that such a union could only bring lasting sorrow.

"I believe you've placed me in a delicate position. I have no right to decide what you should do. That's up to you. But what I can do is share how I see the reality of this situation. Fair enough?"

Tudor and Mura nodded in agreement. Maria continued:

"Mr. Tudor, you have a house in Copăceni. Tell me—does it has electricity?"

"No."

"A bathroom with hot and cold water?"

"No."

"Who does your laundry?"

"Sometimes I do it myself, and sometimes my aunt—my mother's sister—does it."

"You see, Mura" Maria said, "in Copăceni, you won't have

any help. You'll have to do all these things yourself—drawing water from the well in the middle of the yard, lighting the heart, cooking, cleaning, mending, and everything else that needs to be done. Of course, Tudor will help you too, but he has to go to the school—he's the village teacher. He'll also need to tend to the animals and the poultry, to plow the fields, and in summer, to mow the hay. And you'll have to help him. All of that is good, honest work, nothing wrong with it—but you've never done anything like it. You grew up in a palace, and you've always had everything provided for you. Do you think it will be easy to take on all of that? And what about when you have a child? Or two?"

Mura lowered her gaze to the floor. Tudor looked at Maria, heartbroken, seeing all his hopes crumble like a house of cards. He could see so much truth in what the princess was saying. You can't hitch a racehorse to a plow, just like you can't yoke a bull to a cart on a country road. How had he not seen this himself?

Maria went on:

"My aunt, Carmen Sylva, once had a niece whose noble parents died when she was just a child. Moved by the orphan's fate, my aunt took her in and raised her herself, joyfully discovering more of the girl's remarkable qualities—her talent, her love of art and music, and of everything Romanian. She loved the girl so much that she wished to tie her to the family forever, and arranged for her to marry her brother's son, Prince Wilhelm of Wied—a union that came about without difficulty. Now that a new state has formed in the Balkans—Albania—our diplomats are working to convince the great powers to offer its throne to Prince Wilhelm. And I believe they will succeed. That little orphan may soon become a queen. Mura, you know that I have loved you like my own children. I am trying to find such an opportunity for you."

When Maria finished her story, none of them could find the strength to speak. For Tudor, that day perfectly symbolized his downfall—just as Icarus fell for daring to fly too close to the sun. That very day, he had been declared well again, freed from his ravaging illness; he had glimpsed the image of unexpected happiness. But just as he reached for it, fate snatched it away—first his friend, and now, everything else. Like in a game of chance played with fate itself, he had lost everything that had only just begun to take shape in the dreams of that morning.

In his silent gaze, a battle raged between the rising tide of tears and the manly pride that tried to hold them back.

Mura, shaken by the turn of events, found herself unable to choose between the love she felt for this good man and the logic of her lady's arguments—arguments she knew came from a place of deep care. She didn't dare look at Tudor, ashamed of her own weakness, nor at the princess, who was waiting to see how she would react. As if her eyelids weighed tons, she fixed her eyes on the bare floor beneath Tudor's bed.

For a long time, no one had the strength to say the first word. Finally, Maria broke the silence:

"It's late. This has been a dreadful day, full of pain and suffering for each of us. We need rest; since nothing can be resolved tonight, let's go to bed. With God's help, maybe tomorrow we'll find the inspiration for better solutions."

After the women left, Tudor remained in the same position, leaning against the headboard, until late into the night when his eyelids finally closed on their own and he fell into a short, restless sleep—broken by the throbbing pain of his wounds, both in his leg and in his heart.

The Memorial Service

"And I spoke green of twin fir trees –

But beyond the distant groves

Lie my brothers in their droves,

Felled by cholera's cruel sheaves,

Buried thousands, endless grieves –

May the Lord grant them reprieve!"

(*Old folksong, 1913*)

Sunday morning, September 7, 1913. Maria had asked Nando to come to Zimnicea,[xxxvii] so they could attend together a large memorial service in honor of those who could not be saved from the grip of the merciless epidemic.

After placing a flower on each grave on behalf of the mothers, wives, or sisters of the departed, the princely couple stood before the soldiers, gathered in a wide formation on the field that had borne silent witness to the sufferings of each of them.

There, on that very field, the great memorial was held, followed by a *Te Deum* in thanksgiving to the Lord for helping them put an end to the epidemic. It was a splendid day, with bright sunshine, priests robed in golden vestments, church hymns of praise, and the joy of victory—not just on the battlefield, but over cholera itself.

It was a day of celebration, not only because it was a holy Sunday, but because it was a solemn festival echoing deeply within each soul—a day of farewell to that dreadful place, to their fellow men who had endured the same torments and with whom they had forged bonds of brotherhood, and most of all, to the radiant beings who had fought so bravely to wrench them from death's grasp.

Above all, it was a farewell to the one who had inspired them to fight, to endure, to resist, and to triumph over the plague—the one who knew how to soothe, how to comfort, and how to bring them— day after day—a ray of hope that all would end well and they would soon return home.

That day marked Princess Maria's farewell to the cholera camp at Zimnicea. Only a few sufferers remained there; the epidemic that had once ravaged the place was now all but extinguished, and what work remained was in competent and trustworthy hands.

"When the ceremony ended, I slowly passed in front of all those assembled in that wide square formation and placed a flower on each chest—officers, doctors, orderlies, soldiers, row after row—

so that not one was left without a bit of color pinned to his tunic on that day of farewell. And as I moved down the line, all the soldiers erupted into cheers, their young voices rising like a choir toward the heavens. But my eyes filled with tears as I thought of those, I had watched die, who would never return to the arms of their loved ones," wrote Maria in her book: The Story of My Life.

Tudor Avădanei stood among the ranks, propped up on crutches. When Maria reached him, she chose a red rose from the bouquet Mura held and, with her own hand, slipped it through a buttonhole on Tudor's tunic. Their eyes met—sad, glistening, silent—as they said their unspoken goodbye. After the princess and her entourage had moved on, Maria turned once more to look back, a final parting glance, then made her way to the waiting car. The days spent in that place had changed her profoundly; they had forced her to see, to feel, and to judge the world around her in an entirely different light. She was no longer the same woman who had arrived in Zimnicea.

This process of sudden, intense maturation was so powerful that leaving the camp now felt like parting from someone deeply dear—much like the day she had stepped off the royal train and left her family behind to come to Romania in 1893. It was clear to her now: the young men in that camp were part of her family. *They were her family.*

Left alone, Tudor limped slowly toward Izu's grave. When he reached it, he sat on the bare ground, removed the rose from his tunic, and laid it next to the one Maria had placed earlier. Resting his elbows on his good knee, he gazed long into the distance. He wanted to say something, but no words came. He understood this was another farewell—he would never return here again—and that thought weighed heavily on him. It hurt him to know that now no one would stop at this grave again, the place where Izu lay.

Izu had been like a brother. Tudor had cherished their time together, listening to his stories, admiring the wisdom in his words, the ingenuity that helped them find food when there was none, a place to sleep, a way to make life bearable. Maybe it was these very qualities that had stirred envy among others in the unit—and led to his death.

Tudor wanted to tell him—as if Izu could still hear—that he had found a girl he loved, and that in his worst days of suffering, she had stayed by his side, comforting him like an angel. She had wanted to be his wife, but fate had ripped her from him like a hair torn from healthy flesh. But now, his pain was so great that nothing could soothe it. He had no one left to confide in. That's why he came here, to sit with his friend Izu. He would understand.

No. He would not cry. He didn't cry even at Vasilica's grave, though the pain then had been just as sharp—and had never fully left him. The wounds had piled up, one on top of another, emotional on top of physical. Life was full of pain, you got used to it, carried it on your back until you stumbled, and then you were free. That's life, my friend. You're beyond it now. You're free.

"Farewell, Izu. Rest in God's peace. Amen!"

Epilogue

The number of victims of the cholera epidemic in the Romanian army during the 1913 war is estimated at around 1,600 deaths out of approximately 15,000 infected soldiers. Among the civilian population, out of 5,700 reported cases, there **were 3,000 deaths**. It is worth noting that Romania was the first country in the world to combat a cholera epidemic in an organized, scientific manner, making extensive use of the anti-cholera vaccine.

The week following the memorial service at Zimnicea brought with it a new national tragedy. On September 13, 1913, the aircraft *Vlaicu II*, piloted by its inventor Aurel Vlaicu, crashed near Câmpina as he attempted—for the first time—to fly over the Carpathian Mountains on route to his native village, Binținți, in Transylvania.

The death of engineer Aurel Vlaicu was mourned not only throughout Romania but also abroad. He was one of the pioneers of aviation, a man whose work had opened the path to global exploration by air. He was buried at Bellu Cemetery in Bucharest.

After leaving Zimnicea, Sister Pucci, along with the foreign nurses who had worked in the cholera camp with unwavering dedication and self-sacrifice, were invited to the Royal Palace, where they received decorations of honor. As a token of gratitude and appreciation, each was gifted a doll dressed in traditional Romanian costume—with embroidered blouse and skirt, sash, peasant shoes, and headscarf—offered personally by Princess Maria.

As misfortune seldom comes alone, on December 27, Princess Antonia, the mother of Prince Ferdinand, passed away in Sigmaringen. She was dearly loved for her intelligence, grace, and kindness, and her death caused Nando deep sorrow. Maria accompanied him to the funeral, attended by members of numerous European royal houses who came to pay tribute to a woman once famed for her youthful beauty.

On January 4, 1914, at 6:00 p.m., in the library of the Royal Palace in Bucharest, the new Liberal government led by Ionel I.C. Brătianu was sworn in before King Carol I.[xxxviii]

At that time, the king's loyalty to the Triple Alliance was under great strain. The Austro-Hungarian government continued to violate the rights of the Romanian population in Transylvania, ignoring protests from the Romanian government. Even on the international stage, Hungary openly campaigned against Romania. King Carol had appealed to Germany, his diplomatic ally, to intervene on Romania's behalf. Despite promises, nothing changed.

Though an unwavering supporter of the secret treaty with the

Central Powers, it became increasingly clear that public sympathy was shifting toward the Franco-Russian alliance. Offended by the lack of respect shown by his allies, the king began to let events take their course, a stance that only further encouraged the spread of Franco-Russian propaganda among the Romanian population.

On June 28, 1914, the Sarajevo assassination took place. Archduke Franz Ferdinand of Austria and his wife were killed, triggering a political cataclysm that shook all of Europe. Austria demanded the extradition of the assassin from Serbia. Relying on its treaty with Russia, Serbia refused. In response, Russia declared general mobilization. On July 28, Austria-Hungary declared war on Serbia. Then, on August 1, Germany declared war on Russia, and the following day demanded that Belgium allow German troops to cross its territory in route to France.

Kaiser Wilhelm I, convinced that France could be defeated within four weeks and that Germany would then turn its full might against Russia, was stunned by the resistance he encountered. With support from Britain, the French army held firm, and four years later, Germany collapsed in total defeat.

On August 2, Germany requested that Romania declare general mobilization and join the war against Russia. Take Ionescu, had returned from London, and he warned King Carol I that a German victory would mean the final loss of any hope for the liberation of Romanians in Transylvania. The king, now 75 years old, frail and ailing, convened the Crown Council at Peleș Castle the next day and revealed to the leaders of the two main political parties the existence of Romania's secret treaty with the Central Powers.

King Carol stated that the Romanian people would never accept an alliance with Russia, particularly after the annexation of Bessarabia in 1878. He believed that remaining neutral would destroy Romania's international prestige, and therefore, joining the Central Powers was the only viable path. In the middle of the meeting, the Italian diplomat present announced that Italy had declared neutrality, which shook the room.

Debate ensued, with voices both for and against joining the war. Prime Minister Ionel Brătianu urged maintaining the peace treaty signed in Bucharest, insisting that Romania's army was not yet ready for war. He proposed neutrality, with a possible shift toward the Entente Powers (France, Britain, Russia) if they would guarantee Transylvania's unification with Romania.

Following the conference, King Carol's popularity plummeted. Rumors spread that he intended to abdicate and return to his homeland. No one knew how Ferdinand would respond if called to take the throne, a prospect that deeply troubled Maria. Friends and political figures pleaded with her to remain in the country no matter what happened—the hopes of the Romanian people rested on her.

Alarmed by Romania's neutral stance, Austria and Germany sent envoys to pressure the country to act. On September 23, 1914, Count Ottokar Czernin, representing Austria, arrived in Bucharest accompanied by his aide-de-camp, a young noble Hussar officer named Miklós Nádasdy, to speak with the King. Too ill to handle the matter himself, King Carol sent them to speak with Crown Prince Ferdinand.

Ferdinand, careful not to cause complications for the aging monarch, adopted a cautious, noncommittal stance. His reserved and vague responses left Count Czernin dissatisfied and frustrated.

Not long after this audience, on October 9, 1914, King Carol I died in his sleep at Peleş Castle. The next morning, Ferdinand and Maria returned to Sinaia by train, where they were greeted at the station by a jubilant crowd. Cries of "Long live King Ferdinand! Long live Queen Maria!" erupted spontaneously.

King Carol I was given a state funeral, attended by grieving representatives of the Romanian people and envoys from across Europe. He was laid to rest in the sacred grounds of Curtea de Argeş Monastery. Wishing to remain close to her husband, Queen Elisabeth moved into the episcopal palace in Curtea de Argeş, where she awaited the end of her days. It came on March 2, 1916, when she succumbed to galloping pneumonia. Queen Maria was by her side during her final moments. Elisabeth was buried next to her husband in the monastery.

On September 28, 1914, Ferdinand solemnly swore his oath in the Chamber of Deputies, his voice choked with emotion. Queen Maria, dressed in mourning, stood beside him surrounded by four of their six children, and presented her husband with a golden chalice, inscribed with the words: *"Tomorrow may be yours, if your hand is strong enough to grasp it."*[xxxix]

In the twenty-five years since his arrival in Romania, the people knew very little, if anything at all, about their new king. Reserved and deeply shy, Ferdinand had carefully avoided causing his uncle, King Carol, any trouble. He refrained from making public statements, steered clear of political affairs, and kept his distance from court intrigues. As a result, some began to doubt his abilities, even making jokes at his expense, believing they were dealing with a simpleton.

In truth, Ferdinand's intellect surpassed anyone in his circle, far more so than his predecessor, King Carol, who, beyond his military prowess, disciplined character, and sound political instincts, had little else to offer. Ferdinand's military knowledge was precise and highly advanced, and his profound sense of duty to the people he had sworn to serve guided his decisions. He remained loyal to the Romanian nation throughout his life, always giving more than he received—generously, without bitterness or regret. His only flaw was a hesitation to make prompt decisions or give direct orders.

As for Queen Maria, the public's perception of her stood in stark contrast to that of her husband. She was well-known, deeply respected, and genuinely beloved. A widespread belief took root that she was the true leader of the country, and that the king's decisions were, in fact, guided by her counsel. As a result, all eyes turned to her, both in matters of domestic policy and international affairs.

While Romania remained neutral amid the escalating conflict in Europe, Prime Minister Ionel Brătianu, aware of Queen Maria's family ties to the imperial houses of London and St. Petersburg, asked her to communicate Romania's situation to them. He urged her to speak of the Romanian people's aspirations, and, above all, to emphasize how crucial it was to secure a guarantee of support for the unification of Transylvania with Romania, should the country join the war against the Central Powers.

At the same time, out of caution and to avoid arousing suspicion, the government's most important meetings were held in secret, under the guise of private gatherings at the homes of boyars in the capital. Moreover, because all members of Parliament and the government were staunchly pro-Entente, Brătianu, seeking to avoid creating suspicion abroad, appointed several politicians to make fierce public declarations in support of the Triple Alliance, as though impatiently awaiting King Ferdinand's confirmation of the treaty's validity.

Pressure from Germany and Austria-Hungary multiplied in various forms. Alarmed by Queen Maria's influence over her husband, the German minister, von dem Bussche, urged Wilhelm of Hohenzollern to write to his brother Ferdinand, invoking the example of the late King Carol and his loyalty as a true German. Von dem Bussche also summoned Field Marshal von der Goltz to Bucharest to persuade the king to abandon neutrality.

Soon afterward, a new envoy arrived at Cotroceni — Maria's brother-in-law, Prince Hohenlohe-Langenburg — bearing similar messages. Unlike Bussche, Austria's Count Czernin, far more refined, courteous, and diplomatic, requested an audience with Queen Maria, hoping to understand what was keeping Romania neutral. Maria replied that the king, bound by the constitution, was obliged to follow the national will of his people, who demanded neutrality. During the visit, the Austrian official asked for the queen's permission for his young aide-de-camp, Count Miklós Nádasdy, to invite Miss Mura — whom he had met during a previous visit — to a concert. Pleased, the queen agreed.

In the following weeks, Mura became the subject of the young hussar's persistent courtship. He invited her to the opera, concerts, Austrian embassy functions in Bucharest, and several balls.

One evening in the last days of March 1915, as night fell, a car pulled up in front of Father Pârvu's church in Copăceni. A young woman stepped out and entered the candle-lit church. Aside from a few elderly women praying before the icons, their colors faded by years of smoke, the church was empty. She exited through the side door leading to the courtyard and knocked on the priest's house. Father Pârvu appeared, curious to see who it was.

"Good evening, Father! I'm sorry to trouble you. I'm looking for Mr. Tudor Avădanei, and I know you can help me."

"Of course. But what's happened?"

"I cared for him during the cholera outbreak in Zimnicea. I'd like to see him…"

"Certainly! Come inside for a moment — I can't go out just like this. And my wife is here, too. I need to let her know I'm leaving," said the priest, gesturing for her to come in.

Mura stepped inside. The room had woven rugs on the floor, a divan lined with cushions along the wall, an old wardrobe with drawers and doors, a covered table with a large oil lamp in the center, and another lamp hanging on the wall. The priest's wife appeared in the kitchen doorway to see who the guest was and asked her to wait — the priest would be ready in a moment.

When they returned to the street, a crowd gathered around the car, eager to see who had arrived. Father Pârvu made his way through them with a sense of importance and took his seat beside Mura in the front. When they arrived at Tudor's house, they entered the yard. Tudor appeared in the doorway, leaning on a cane.

"Mura? You're here?"

Mura rushed into his arms without saying a word. From the back of the yard, Aunt Ileana appeared, one hand pressed to her chest, the other covering her mouth, unsure what to make of it. Father Pârvu made the sign of the cross. Tudor wrapped his free arm around the girl's shoulders, waiting to hear what had happened. After a brief moment, Mura looked up into Tudor's eyes:

"Do you still love me?"

"Of course I do! What kind of question is that?"

"Then marry me! Now. Right now."

"All right! But tell me, what's going on?"

"No. There's no time! Father is here — I want us to be married now. We must be married now!"

Tudor looked at Father Pârvu, who was just as stunned as he was.

"Well, what can I say? Let's go back to the church… Let Aunt Ileana come with us too, as a witness," the priest said.

"How can I come like this, Father? I must get dressed properly first!" Aunt Ileana objected.

"No! There's no time to waste. I'll explain later," Mura insisted, pulling Tudor by the hand toward the gate.

They all went to church. The priest slipped behind the altar to gather the necessary vestments. Tudor went to fetch the priest's wife, whose signature was needed as a witness. Everyone gathered in front of the iconostasis, waiting for the priest to appear. Mura squeezed Tudor's hand.

"Will you love me for the rest of your life?"

Tudor smiled. His eyes were wet.

"Will you always be as mysterious as you are now?"

"No. I'm afraid Her Majesty may try to stop us again. I believe she's already on my trail."

Tudor answered by squeezing her hand tighter. Father Pârvu returned in full vestments, holding crowns and a golden chalice. Under one arm, he carried an old Bible, its corners worn and curling with age. Chanting the prayers in his nasal, hoarse voice, he solemnly performed the wedding ceremony, binding together two souls whose vows flickered like the candle flames around them.

After the service, the priest turned to his wife:

"So, mamaie, have you got something good prepared so we can celebrate the children's wedding?"

"Well, I think I can rustle up some cheese, eggs, sausages… and a drop or two of wine!"

Tudor and Mura remained in each other's embrace beneath the dome of the Copăceni church, isolated from the others in a world of their own. When they saw the rest of the group heading toward the priest's house, they, too, moved to follow. Tudor felt as though he were dreaming—everything seemed so unreal, as if such things could happen only to him. But at that very moment, just as Mura had feared, Her Majesty Queen Marie appeared in the church, accompanied by two officers.

"Is it possible you would shame me like this, Mura? After all I've done for you?"

"Ma'am, I had no other choice! You have no idea what's unfolding behind Your Majesty's back… I cannot be part of this conspiracy!"

"What conspiracy? Come with me, you can tell me on the way!"

"No, ma'am! It's too late! I'm married to Tudor!"

"What are you saying? When did you get married?" Maria

asked, astonished.

"Ten minutes ago. The priest here in Copăceni performed the ceremony. We had witnesses."

Maria looked disapprovingly at the faces around her. There stood Tudor before her, leaning on his cane. Mura, upright like a candle, had found the strength to face her—and the Queen couldn't imagine what wrong she had done to deserve such rebellion. She had only ever wanted the best for her.

"Did I do something wrong? Why did you feel the need to take revenge on me?" Maria asked.

"No, Your Majesty! This isn't revenge!" Mura protested. "I had to do this. I cannot belong to people who seek to profit from an alliance with me. They don't want me, they want to use me to find out what you do, what you think, who you speak with. I'm not a spy, and that's what they want me to be!"

Mura began to cry. This time, she could no longer hold back the pain that had been nesting in her soul ever since she realized that every conversation with the young hussar, and everyone she met in his circle, was riddled with probing questions about the Queen's life—her daily routine, her habits, her children, her discussions with others. Even the smallest details were picked apart with further questions, all cloaked in light-hearted amusement and childish smiles. Now, Mura regretted not having realized from the start that she had been lured in by the glittering attention of prominent figures. Perhaps, out of vanity, she had let slip things she shouldn't have, until she finally understood what they were after.

At last, the Queen understood. She saw that Mura had been right. Out of fear that she might be forced to meet such people again, Mura had come here and married Tudor. Through this act, perhaps even a sacrifice, she had put an end to any further attempts to marry her off to someone else. Her decision was final and irreversible. Moved, Maria stepped forward and embraced her. Mura let herself be held.

"You're not angry with me?"

"My dear child, how could I be angry? I'm grateful to you! Perhaps we're not yet able to understand just how great a service you've done for us, how much suffering you've spared us, and how deeply I valued you for it."

Maria led Mura to where Tudor stood, having watched the scene unfold from nearby.

"I'm glad you're finally together! I wish you both a happy life, eternal love, and healthy children! Go to the manor in Copăceni and make it your home! I'll gladly come visit. Farewell and be well!"

As she turned to leave, Father Pârvu appeared at the side

door:

"Well, aren't you coming? The food's getting cold…"

He stopped short when he saw the Queen standing inside his own church.

"Your Majesty don't go! I've long wished for the chance to bow at your feet for all you've done. Please, stay a little while longer! Look—these young ones I've just married, and my wife's prepared some refreshments. Please, stay!"

Maria stopped in her tracks. She exchanged a glance with the two officers accompanying her, then smiled at the priest and said:

"Well then, we can't leave the good priestess waiting, can we?"

THE END

About The Author

Born in Bucharest, Romania, in January 1934, David Kimel witnessed the changes and turmoil of his country, dragged by forces beyond its control in the era preceding, during, and after the Second World War. Raised on the periphery of the city, surrounded by poor to middle-class neighbors, he learned at an early age the existence of prejudice, the lessons of survival which kept his Jewish family afloat through tough times, and gave him the strength to grow as a man.

After finishing an industrial school, he was selected by the Romanian Writers Union in 1952 for a scholarship at "Școala de Literatură și Critică Literară Mihail Eminescu," an eminent literary academy for young writers, where he had the opportunity to meet the most prominent writers as teachers and colleagues. But he couldn't satisfy the regime's requirements and found work in industry. He married, had children, and immigrated to Canada in 1975, after a waiting period of eight months for a visa in a Greece refugee camp.

In his new country, he obtained a designer job with Magna International, a multinational company for automotive parts, where he held a leading position until retirement. He started to write again when his children became young adults. Among the many publications where he began collaborating, *Observatorul* (The

235

Observer), a Romanian magazine in Toronto, created a permanent column, "Subjective," where his articles have appeared regularly for almost 20 years.

Many books in English and Romanian featuring his name have been printed since 2008. Among them, *Simple Seeds*, a poetry book printed by Author House, and *A Foggy Sunrise*, published by iUniverse. Other books, *A Sweetless Love,* and *In the Pursuit of Happiness*, together with a new edition of "A Foggy Sunrise" are presently ready for sale on Amazon, Apple, Google and Goodreas.

Many books printed in Romania and Canada are available to Romanian readers: *Domnița și Tudor Avădanei,* an historic novel, *Capcana,* also a novel, the short story books named *În Căutarea Fericirii* and *Anișoara. Flori de Toamnă* for the poetry lovers, *Zori Încețoșate,* an autobiography expanding as a true novel, *Din Lumea Largă*, a travelogue through many countries, and a collection of published articles, *Disecarea Timpului Prezent.*

David Kimel is a member of the Romanian Writers Association of Canada (ASRC), the Writers and Editors Network, and the recipient of a Second Prize in the International Competition of Saga Printing House for the short story titled *Domnul Bratu.*

Notes

[i] Carol 1, King of Romania, (1839-1914), born Karl, Prince of Hohenzollern-Sigmaringen. Married with Elisabeth, Princess of Wied.

[ii] Ferdinand 1, King of Romania, (1865-1927), Nando, born Prince of Hohenzollern-Sigmaringen, son of Leopold, the older brother of king Carol I. Married with Maria, Princess of Edinburg.

[iii] Ion I. C. Brătianu, (1864-1927) prominent politician, five times Prim-minister of Romania and lieder of The National Liberal Party, son of I.C. Brătianu.

[iv] Maria, Queen of Romania, (1875-1938), Missy, born Princess of Edinburg, daughter of Alfred, Duke of Edinburg and Maria Alexandrova, Duchess of Edinburg and Coburg. Married with Ferdinand 1, King of Romania.

[v] Ioan Kalinderu, (1840-1913), The Royal Domains Administrator, Personal Counsellor to King Carol 1 and member of Romanian Academy.

[vi] Ion C. Brătianu, (1822-1891), politician, active participant at 1848 Romanian Revolution, former Prim-minister, lieder of The National Liberal Party, and instrumental in bringing Prince Carol de Hohenzollern-Sigmaringen, as voivode of Romania.

[vii] Nicolae Filipescu, (1862-1916), Romanian politician, former Mayor of Bucharest and Minister of War in the Conservative Government leaded by Peter Carp. He redacted Epoca, a daily newspaper, and lead the National Front of Action to join Romania in First World War with Antanta.

[viii] Elena Văcărescu, (1864-1947), Frech writer, member of Romanian Academy and Ambassador at the Ligue of United Nation

[ix] Maria Alexandrova, (1853-1920), Maria's mother, Princess of Great Brithany, Duchess of Edinburg and Saxa-Coburg Gotha, born Grand Duchess and daughter of Tzar Alexander II of Russia.

[x] Wilhelm II, (1859-1941), Kaizer of Germany, Maria's first grade cousin, accused of escalation of World War I and defeat of Germany.

xi Elisabeth, Queen of Romania, (1843-1916), born Princess of Wied, married with King Carol I of Romania. Known as The Poet Queen, Carmen Sylva.

xii Maria, Queen of Romania – The Story of My Life – vol I, page 203, Editura Eminescu 1991

xiii Maria, Queen of Romania – The Story of My Life – vol II, page 24, Editura Eminescu 1991

xiv Maria, Queen of Romania – The Story of My Life – vol II, page 25, Editura Eminescu 1991

xv George Enescu, (1881-1955), Romanian composer, violinist, pianist, conductor and teacher, renown as greatest musician in Romanian history. Maria, Queen of Romania – The Story of My Life – vol II, page 110, Editura Eminescu 1991

xvi Take Ionescu, (1858-1922), Romanian politician, partisan of Romania participation in Balkan's Wars and ally to Antanta coalition in the 1st World War. Diplomat and brilliant orator.

xvii Titu Maiorescu, (1840-1917), Romanian politician, literary critique who founded Societatea *Junimea* (Junimea Literary Circle), Prim-minister in Balkan Wars period.

xviii Maria, Queen of Romania – The Story of My Life – vol II, page 120, Editura Eminescu 1991

xix Maria, Queen of Romania – The Story of My Life – vol II, page 122, Editura Eminescu 1991

xxi Hannah Pacula, Queen of Romania, page 80, Eland 1984.

xxii Hannah Pacula, Queen of Romania, page 81, Eland 1984.

xxiii Wikipedia: The Republic of Ploiești.

xxiv Hannah Pacula, Queen of Romania, page 83, Eland 1984.

xxv Wikipedia: Carol I of Romania.

xxvi Neagu Djuvara, (1916-2018), Romanian historian, A Concise History of Romania, page 233, Cross Meridian 2012

xxvii Barbu Aexandru Ştirbei, (1872-1946), The Royal Domains Administrator, Personal Counsellor to King Ferdinand I and Queen Maria.

xxviii Elisa Brăteanu, (1870-1957), Barbu Ştirbei's sister, philanthrope, provided war ambulatory hospitals, patron of nurses' schools and participant of Women Delegation to the Lique of Nations.

xxix Wikipedia: Romanian military equipment of World War I

[xxx] Wikipedia: Cholera Epidemy during Romanian participation to second Balkan War.
[xxxi] Maria, Queen of Romania – The Story of My Life – vol II, page 359, Editura Eminescu 1991
[xxxii] Maria, Queen of Romania – The Story of My Life – vol II, page 363, Editura Eminescu 1991
[xxxiii] Wikipedia: Cholera Epidemy during Romanian participation to second Balkan War.
[xxxiv] I.G.Duca, Political Memoirs, Vol. I, Page12
[xxxv] I.G.Duca, Political Memoirs, Vol. I, Page15
[xxxvi] Wikipedia: Cholera Epidemy during Romanian participation to second Balkan War.
[xxxvii] Maria, Queen of Romania – The Story of My Life – vol II, page 365, Editura Eminescu 1991
[xxxviii] I.G.Duca, Political Memoirs, Vol. I, Page16
[xxxix] Maria, Queen of Romania – The Story of My Life – vol II, page 410, Editura Eminescu 1991

Selected Bibliography

1. *Maria Regina României – Povestea Vieţii Mele* – vol. I, II, III. Editura Eminescu

2. Hannah Pakula – *Queen Of Roumania – The life of Princess Marie, grand daughter of Queen Victoria,* Eland, 1989

3. Neagu Djuvara – *A coincise History of Romanians,* Cross Medium, 2012

4. I. G. Duca – *Amintiri Politice* – vol. I Colecţia „Memorii şi Mărturii" Jon

Dumitru-Verlag, Munchen, 1981

5. *Carol I of Romania* – https://en.m.wikipedia.org/wiki/Carol_I_of_ Romania

6. *Republica de la Ploieşti* – https://ro.m.wikipedia.org/wuki/Repu blica_ de_la_Ploieşti

7. *Ferdinand I of Romania* – https://en.m.wikipedia.org/wiki/ Ferdinand_ I_of_Romania

8. *Marie of Romania* – https://en.m.wikipedia.org/wiki/Marie_of_Romania

9. *Tripla Alianţă (1882)* – https://ro.m.wikipedia.org/wiki/Tripla_Alianţă_ (1882)

10. *1907 Romanian peasants' revolt* – https://ro.wikipedia.org/wiki/R%C4%83scoala_%C8%9A%C4%83r %C4%83neasc%C4%83_din_1907

11. *FirstBalcan War* – https://en.m.wikipedia.org/wiki/First_Balcan_War

12. *Al Doilea Război Balcanic* – https://ro.m.wikipedia.org/wiki/Al_Doilea_ Război_Balcanic

13. *Romanian militaryequipment of World War I* – https://en.m.wikipedia. org/wiki/Romanian_militaru_equipment_of_world_War_I

14. *Tratatul de la Bucureşti (1913)* – https://ro.m.wikipedia.org/wiki/ Tratatul_de_la_Bucureşti_ (1913)

15. *Second Balcan War* – https://en.m.wikipedia.org/wiki/Second_Balcan_ War

16. *Epidemia de holeră din timpul participării României la cel de-Al Doilea Război Balcanic* –
https://ro.m.wikipedia.org/wiki/Epidemia_de_ho -
leră_din_timpul_participarii_Romaniei_la_cel_de-Al_Doilea_
Război_ Balcanic
17. Andrei Pogăciaş – *Tratatul de pace de la Bucureşti din 1913 şi consecinţele sale*
18. *Ottoman Empire declares a holywar* – *This day in History* – November 14, 1914.
19. *Piloţi români în cel de-al doilea război balcanic* (Galerie Foto) –
https://m.ziuaconstanta.ro/arhive/citestedobrogea/citeste...-cel-deal-doilea-razboi-balcanic-galerie-foto-801769.html
20. Ciprian Dragnea – *Marşul „ Drum bun"* – Utube.
21. *Regina Maria a României – între pasiune şi raţiune,* în „ Poveste vieţii mele" – https://www.argesexpres.ri/index.php/cultura/13324-regina-romaniei-între-pasiune-şi-ratiune-in-povestea-vietii-mele-ii
22. *Alexandru B. Ştirbei* – https://en.m.wikipedia.org/wiki/Alexandru_
B_Ştirbei
23. *Take Ionescu* – https://en.m.wikipedia.org/wiki/Take_Ionescu
24. *Ion Cantacuzino* – https://ro.m.wikipedia.org/wiki/Ion_Cantacuzino
25. *Alexandru Marghiloman* – ttps://en.m.wikipedia.org/wiki/Alexandru
_Marghiloman
26. *Marthe Bibesco* – https://en.m.wikipedia.org/wiki/Marthe_Bibesco
27. *Short History of Bucharest: From the Medieval Centuries to Communism*– https://www.uncover-romania.com/attractions/cities/history-ofbucharest
28. *Conacul Reginei Maria* – https://www.forbes.ro/comori-arhitecturale--conacul-reginei maria-proiectat-de-arh-paul-gottereau-2-219216
29. *În inima Bucureştiului, pe Magheru, era cândva un fabulos templu grecesc: Muzeul Simu* – https://b.365.ro/in-inima-bucurestiului-pemagheru-era-c...gYSdOacQnwGpJLAxgPBOt-Tf6Vsk#I7b5pxOy26ay16aed1t
30. *O vizită la Hipodromul Băneasa* – https://viabucuresti.ro/o-vizita-lahipodromul-baneasa/
31. *Romanian Athenaeum* –https://en.m.wikipedia.org/wiki/Romanian_
Athenaeum
32. *Castelul Peleş* – https://ro.m.wikipedia.org/wiki/Castelul_Peleş

33. *Povestea Palatului Cotroceni* – https://b365.ro/povestea-palatuluicotroceni-casa-domnit...J8ibjkRCkiUhCTIqvuEVA7DGR9_ONFc#I73bIdn9q3uw6xuspa
34. *Elisabeta Palace* – https://en.m.wikipedia.org/wiki/Elisabeta_Palace
35. *Aruncătură de băţ de Bucureşti,* de Filip Lupşa – https://b365.ro/povestea-palatului-stirbey-superbul-dome...t2G94EQyY_jELnGp86U5XY2AHAVQ#I6v6buw8f7o2ypj22k5
36. *Mogoşoaia Palace* – https://en.m.wikipedia.org/wiki/Mogoşoaia_Palace

Glossary

a: In Romanian Language **a** is pronounce like **a** in **a**dd, m**a**p.

e: is pronounce like **e** in **e**nd, p**e**t.

i: is pronounce like **i** in **i**t, g**i**ve

o: is pronounce like **o** in **o**dd, h**o**t.

u: is pronounce like **oo** in p**oo**l, f**oo**d.

ă: is pronounce like **a** in **a** dollar, **a**bout.

â: is pronounce like **i** in g**i**rl, g**i**rdle.

ș: is pronounce like **sh** in **sh**ore, **sh**ould.

ț: is pronounce like **tz** in **tz**ar, **tz**igane.

ce: is pronounce like **ch** in **ch**erry, **ch**ain.

ci: is pronounce like **ch** in **ch**icken, **ch**in.

chi: is pronounce like **k** in **k**ing, **k**ill.

che: is pronounce like **k** in **k**eg, **k**ernel.

ge: is pronounce like **g** in **g**el, **g**em.

gi: is pronounce like **g** in **g**ee, **g**in.

ghe: is pronounce like **g** in **g**et, **g**eyser.

ghi: is pronounce like **g** in **g**ift, **g**ive.

Domniţa, pag. 4 – Grand Lady, Princess, a name given to a maiden of ruling class.

Avădanei, pag. 4 – "a vădanei"- off a widow woman

Conu', pag. 11 – "conul" – a title given to a person who possess a large estate.

Nene (Tanti), pag. 16 – uncle (aunt), respectful terms used to address an older man (woman), even when they are not related.

Martha Bibescu (1886-1973)**,** pag. 52 – Romanian – French writer, socialite, known for literary work and social involvement.

Muzeul Simu, pag. 52 – built in 1910 by Anastasie Simu, a famous art collector, in the center of Bucharest city in the form of an antic Greek temple. His entire art collection was exposed there and donated to Romanian people. In 1961, the communist regime destroyed the museum considering it a manifestation of decadent culture.

Stolnic, pag. 56 – a title of nobles given to a person in charge of the royal table in medieval Romanian court.

The Cernavoda Bridge, pag. 73 - build by engineer Anghel Saligny in 1895 over the Danube River, connecting Romania Country to formerly Bulgarian Dobruja region added to Romania in 1878 in exchange for Bessarabia lands taken by Russia after the war against Ottoman Empire in 1877. It was considered the longest bridge in Europe and second in the World.

Birth of Romania: pag. 95 – In 1858 the Great European Powers decided to allow Romanian Principalities of Wallachia and Moldavia to share a few common institutions having two rulers. On January 5, 1859, Moldavia choses Alexandru Ion Cuza as their ruler. On January 24, 1859, Wallachia also elected their ruler in the person of Alexandru Ion Cuza. After three years of negotiation the union was accepted for the term of Cuza rule. The United Principalities of Walachia and Moldavia were permitted to use the name of Romania.